PUFFIN BOOKS

Editor: Kaye Webb

FELL FARM FOR CHRISTMAS

The five Brownes, two pairs of twins and young Sally, had the luck to go back to the Fell Farm for Christmas and had a wonderful holiday there with a succession of unusual adventures. Jan, as before, pursued his 'birding' with enthusiasm, and was able to rescue a heron which had got frozen into a pond while it was standing on one leg, fishing. One pair of twins were caught in a blizzard which blew so hard that, next morning, the family woke to find snow almost to the tops of the bedroom windows. Yes, they were certainly good holidays!

Those who read *Fell Farm Holiday* and *Fell Farm Campers* won't need to be told that this story moves briskly from start to finish. They will expect this and won't be disappointed. All three books, by the way, are obtainable only in Puffins. The author has again made her own pictures, but the gay cover design is by Astrid Walford.

MARJORIE LLOYD

FELL FARM
FOR CHRISTMAS

A SEQUEL TO
Fell Farm Holiday

PUFFIN BOOKS

Puffin Books, Penguin Books Ltd, Harmondsworth, Middlesex, England
Penguin Books Inc., 7110 Ambassador Road, Baltimore, Maryland 21207, U.S.A.
Penguin Books Australia Ltd, Ringwood, Victoria, Australia
Penguin Books Canada Ltd, 41 Steelcase Road West,
Markham, Ontario, Canada
Penguin Books (N.Z.) Ltd, 182–190 Wairau Road, Auckland 10, New Zealand

—

First published 1954
Reprinted 1968, 1971, 1975

—

Made and printed in Great Britain
by Cox & Wyman Ltd, London, Reading and Fakenham
Set in Monotype Baskerville

To Elizabeth Lloyd,
my mother
★

CONTENTS

	By Way of Introduction	11
1.	Journey to the Fells	14
2.	Westmorland Again	21
3.	Old Friends Mostly	28
4.	Tally-Ho!	36
5.	View Halloo!	41
6.	Sleuthing Jan	53
7.	Old Nod	59
8.	Christmas Day in the Morning	69
9.	Here We Come A-wassailing	77
10.	A Walk of Some Importance	83
11.	Back After Nightfall	91
12.	Rustlers	98
13.	Daylight Investigation	105
14.	A Medal for Gallantry	116
15.	Birding	124
16.	Then Blizzard	132
17.	A Deepening Depression	142
18.	Indoor Activities	149
19.	Tracks in the Snow	157
20.	Last Day	168

LIST OF ILLUSTRATIONS

'*Do* be a sport, Hyacinth' 12
Aunt Gretchen had seen us off from Euston 14
A last-minute dash by Jan 16
A giddy, whirling ring 24
Winked one little, black eye 30
'Ee, thanks, wur champion!' 33
Mr Tiggle hard on her heels 37
I set to work, too 42
Kay absolutely at his heels 47
'Help, Pat, help!' 51
Looking remarkably innocent 53
Sat there watching 56
'Stop interrupting!' 62
'Good-bye, Old Nod!' 66
Made a clean sweep of the mixing bowls 70
A white elephant with ears as big as rhubarb
   leaves 73
Started on 'The First Nowell' 79
Bagged our usual job 83
'Come on!' Pat hissed 88
Yawning tremendously 94
Saved our wind for the running 96
'This a deputation?' 106
Sat and ate sandwiches 111
Once again collecting local colour 114
'Hasn't touched his milk' 117
Mr Tiggle in her arms 120
'Sally's going to help' 126
'It's the *perfect* bird hide!' 129

Went ahead as planned   135
Three rather shapeless figures   139
Turned our attention to our battle with the
    blizzard   144
Felt his nose with care   147
I fell out of the wheelbarrow   151
Ascent (with ice-axe) of Jackdaw chimney   155
'Sally turns her toes in!'   161
Stood for about five seconds   166
Under Pat's quartermaster eye   169
Last look at all the things that counted   172
'And Easter means – High Tarn?'   173

MAPS

The High Tarn Region   10
Birdwatchers' Route   128

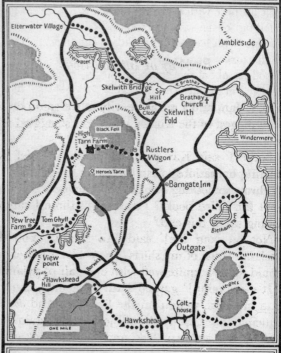

THE HIGH TARN REGION

Elterwater Village
Elterwater
Loughrigg Tarn
Ambleside
Skelwith Bridge
Spy Hill
R. Brathay
Brathay Church
Bull Close
Skelwith Fold
Black Fell
High Tarn Farm
Rustlers Wagon
Windermere
Heron's Tarn
Barngate Inn
Yew Tree Farm
Tom Ghyll
Tarn Hows
Bletham Tarn
Outgate
View point
Borwick
Hawkshead Hill
Claife Heights
Colthouse
ONE MILE
Hawkshead

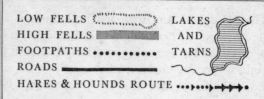

LOW FELLS
HIGH FELLS
FOOTPATHS
ROADS
LAKES
AND
TARNS
HARES & HOUNDS ROUTE

FELL FARM FOR CHRISTMAS

TOLD BY HYACINTH

*

By Way of Introduction

SALLY, Jan, and I sat as heavily as we could on top of the biggest of the trunks, while Pat struggled with the locks.

'Bother!' said Kay (who, as packer-in-chief, was directing operations). 'Isn't it going to fasten?'

'Throw something overboard,' I suggested. 'What about Jan's bird books? I'm sure it's those I can feel pushing up at this end.'

'Not on your life!' said Jan firmly. 'You can chuck out some of my shirts, if you like. Or I expect I could manage quite well with one pair of pyjamas.'

'It's – coming!' gasped Pat. 'Hyacinth, can you put a bit more weight on the far side? And *do* stop bouncing about, Sally. You'll jerk it out again.'

There was a sharp click, and Pat sat back on his heels.

'Good!' sighed Kay with relief. 'I thought I was going to have to begin again from the beginning. Now there's only the roping and labelling, and then, I think, we're absolutely ready.'

'So, at half past nine tomorrow morning –' began Pat.

'– we set out for the fells!' I finished.

'Hurrah!' yelled Jan, while Sally bounced up and down on the trunk with excitement.

'By the way,' said Kay. 'Are we going to keep a journal again this holiday?'

'Ought to.'

'Takes such a *time*,' said Jan unenthusiastically.

'Not of *yours*,' retorted Kay. 'You only did one chapter of the last; and no one made a fuss about your spelling!'

'I've got an idea,' said Pat.

'What?'

'Hyacinth edits it. It's rather up her street, you know.'

'Good notion! That all right for you, Hyacinth?'

'*Might* be,' I said.

'I think it's a *wizard* idea,' said Jan, this time with great enthusiasm.

'Do *be a sport, Hyacinth*'

'It'd be much better done by one person,' said Kay. 'Then we'd be sure it didn't say the same things twice.'

'*Do* be a sport, Hyacinth,' said Pat, knowing quite well that in the end I always give in to his persuasion.

'All right,' I agreed (not really so reluctantly as I made it sound). 'I'll do it. But you'll need to unfasten that trunk again, Pat. I'll have to put in *reams* of paper!'

CHAPTER I

Journey to the Fells

IT is a good thing really that you have met all five of us before, because this time I don't need to bother about introductions, but can begin right away by saying that, once again, we were in the Lakes Express, and heading northwards.

It was the first real day of the Christmas holidays, and Aunt Gretchen had seen us off from Euston. As

Aunt Gretchen had seen us off from Euston

usual she had been a bit anxious about Sally who is just eight, and – being the only one of us who isn't a twin – is the odd man out in our rather odd family. I suppose it *is* a responsibility for Aunt Gretchen, being a sort of guardian to us while Mother and Father are away in India. But I do think that she sometimes gets more worried about it than she need. Sally is really, for her age, quite sensible (with occasional lapses), and Pat and Kay are pretty good at taking care of her. After all, they are fifteen – almost hoary; and Jan and I are only two years younger. Come to think of it, it's Jan who would be Aunt G's biggest worry, if only she knew – and just possibly me. But some things we very wisely keep to ourselves.

So Kay said 'Yes, Aunt Gretchen', to all the instructions. But I'm not sure that she was really listening. There was a sort of far-away look in her eye, and I'm pretty certain that her mind was really on the fells.

But I am wasting time on Euston and the goodbyes. They were very soon over. At ten-twenty-five exactly the guard's whistle shrilled. There were shouts, banging of doors, and some last-minute dashes (one of them by Jan who had decided, thirty seconds earlier, that he simply *must* have the bird magazine which he'd seen on the bookstall). Then, inch by inch, with the most horrible groans and sighs, like a huge, lazy monster, the train began to move. Aunt G had a new anxiety.

'Oh, Kay, you will remember to see that Sally –'

But she was too late. For our monster had found its energy and gathered speed. The rest of the instruction was left far behind on the platform, and we, once again, were heading northwards towards Mr and Mrs Jenks, the fell farm, and all the thousand and one delights to be found there.

It was comfortable and warm inside the carriage, and we discarded our top-coats at once. These and

A last-minute dash by Jan

our gaberdines and rucksacks (absolutely bulging with food until we'd made our successive onslaughts on them) were stacked away on the rack. We always try to have as little luggage actually with us as we can, and to leave ourselves fairly mobile. That's Father's tip, and he is a seasoned traveller. So we carry only the things which will sling on to us.

Of course we don't believe in going up to the fells short of equipment, and that can be pretty bulky – nailed boots, thick socks, wind jackets, and, for a winter holiday, all the extras such as thick pullovers, mitts, and balaclava helmets. But such things were in the luggage van, in the two biggest of our school trunks. It was when these had been packed and roped and, finally, labelled that we felt we could smell the fells again.

> The Family Munro Browne
> Passengers to High Tarn Farm
> Nr Ambleside
> Westmorland
> Via Euston, Crewe, Oxenholme, and Windermere

in Pat's clear, firm printing, seemed to make it all so very certain.

In the rukkers, as well as food, we'd brought things to occupy us during the journey – especially for the first part when it was much too soon to watch for the fells.

Sally had a jig-saw, and bagged the table clamped to the window side. Jan was soon engrossed in his bird magazine, and Pat deep in a book on climbing in the Himalayas. He also practised his sea-knots on a piece of green cord, ready for the time when he goes into the navy, as he intends to do. Luckily Father and Mother both approve of this plan, so he won't need to run away to sea.

Kay divided her time between knitting a pair of socks, and reading her holiday task, which was, I think, *Pride and Prejudice*. It's a funny thing about holiday tasks – the way they put you off, I mean, even when they are things that you would normally read quite happily. So Kay was very wise to be getting on with hers while there wasn't much else to do.

I'd got both my note-books with me, but I put away my poetry one, and set to work on the one in which I'm writing my thriller (*The Mysterious Affair of*

the Blood-stained Hippopotamus), as that seemed the sort
of thing on which I could concentrate during a train
journey. The others haven't yet read any of it. It
would be hard on them to be held up in the middle,
and I'm still not at all sure how it is going to end.
But I've promised Jan that, when he does read it, it
will make even his hair stand on end; so he is keen to
have it finished quickly.

The journey, as usual, started quietly. We spread
ourselves out, to make the carriage look pretty full,
and got on with our separate occupations. It was a
wonderful day, crisp and sparkling as the very best
December days can be, full of colour, and with a
china-blue sky. We thought of the fells, which we
knew would be snow-capped, and simply *ached* to
get to them quickly, before all the brilliance had
faded. But there was nothing we could do about
that, and anyhow sixty-five miles per hour isn't a bad
speed at which to be hurtling towards them. That was
probably quite a fair estimate; Pat made it by timing
with Kay's watch, and counting telegraph poles.

The rukkers had positively bulged to begin. We
had our mid-mornings from them as we sped through
Bletchley, a hearty lunch between Rugby and Crewe,
and a sort of afternoon snack just before Warrington.
It all helped to pass the time. As we drew into Lancaster we really felt that we were on the verge.

'Better start to pack up, hadn't we?' suggested
Kay.

'Ooh, yes! Do let's do it now; then we can concentrate on looking out for landmarks.'

'Bit of a litter, I must say!' Pat is always critical
of things not shipshape. He started to give Sally a

hand with the clearing of the jig-saw. She had finished, very triumphantly (except for the two missing pieces), just before Preston.

'Still,' pointed out Kay, 'the litter's served its purpose. We've only had two invasions the whole way.'

'Do you *really* think it was a ferret that the man who got in at Crewe had in his box?' asked Sally.

'*Certain* it was,' said Jan. 'They always carry them about in those wooden boxes with thick straps that go over their shoulders. Gosh! I'd have given anything to look inside.'

'Huh! Supposing it had got out,' I shivered.

'What would it have done?' demanded Sally. 'Would it – would it have *killed* us?'

'Probably have tried to, if it had been cornered,' said Kay.

'And put the Blood-stained Hippo's nose *right* out of joint!' Pat pitched the rucksacks off the rack. 'Come on, we'll be at Oxenholme in a jiffy, and there'll be no time for anything after that.'

We were somewhere between Hest Bank and Carnforth – the bit where the railway runs along the edge of the sea, and you usually get the first view of the fells, looking simply wonderful across the great curve of the bay.

But this time it was half past four on an afternoon in late December, and the light had gone from the sky, except for some long, dim bars of gold just above the horizon. I swore that I could just glimpse the faintest gleam of snow-caps, pale as silver. The others said that it was imagination, and maybe it was; but it really didn't matter, because we all knew that they were there.

We jumped to, and started to pack away books and papers and knitting and jig-saws and the oddments of fruit that were left. There was now lots of room in the rukkers (especially since we'd eaten an early tea, somewhere between Preston and Lancaster), and it didn't take long to get things stowed away. By the time we pulled into Oxenholme all was shipshape. We'd cleaned up Sally's face a bit; I'd found my missing hair-ribbon, and Kay had re-done one of my plaits. The rukkers were fastened up, with gaberdines strapped on to them; we had got into top-coats, and were clustered at the window side of the carriage – the side that looks towards the west and gets the first glimpse of our own very special fell-tops.

Personally I felt almost sick with excitement. None of the others said anything about it; in fact they were all most unusually quiet. But I'm ready to bet that they felt much the same as I did.

CHAPTER 2

Westmorland Again

THAT last ten miles, from Oxenholme to Windermere, is always the longest part of the journey. The train crawls along for centuries.

I suppose it was mere wishful thinking that made us cluster round the window, with noses to the pane; for, except for one last, crimson streak, the light had completely gone, and we had only the vaguest idea of whether we were passing through cuttings, or between trees, or looking out unseeingly across the high, rocky pastures to the far fells. We made the first stop.

'Kendal!' chirped Sally, very pleased with herself at remembering. It wasn't a difficult guess. That is the only station of any size along the line.

We jerked into motion again, chugged laboriously for a time, then clanked again to a standstill.

'Burneside. Wish we didn't have to stop so often', sighed Jan.

The train seemed to sense our impatience, for it chugged on again in less than two minutes. We pulled up a third time.

'Staveley,' said Pat, 'and here's the ticket collector. You've got them, haven't you, Kay?'

'Hope so! I certainly had them when we started'.

'Awful,' I shuddered, 'if they were lost, and they turned us back at this stage.'

'They wouldn't do that.' (Jan is the family optimist.) 'We'd give our names and address, and say we'd pay tomorrow.'

'But we haven't enough money,' I reminded him.

'Oh, we could always pawn Kay's watch.'

'Well I'm dashed!' exploded Kay.

The ticket collector came along the corridor, so there wasn't time to argue the point – nor any need, for she'd got the tickets quite safely.

'Tick-its, plaase!' said the collector. Then, as they were handed to him, he looked at us over his spectacles.

'Seen you five before, 'aven't I?'

'Mm!' I said. 'Often.'

'Thought so,' said the ticket collector, very satisfied with his feat of memory. 'And I 'ope I'll see you again often. Well now, 'ave a good 'oliday.'

'Thank you very much,' we said in chorus; and I added, 'We hope we'll see you often, too.'

He nodded, and we heard him along the corridor, his 'Tick-its plaase!' getting gradually more distant.

The train came to life with a jerk that sent us all tumbling into a heap in the corner of the engine-facing seat. Jan was at the bottom. I felt that it was a judgement on him for being so airy about Kay's watch.

'Next stop, and we're there,' I said, as we sorted ourselves out. 'D'you think Mr Jenks is on the platform already?'

'Mm! He wouldn't risk being late. And the lorry'll be drawn up at the side entrance.'

'What d'you guess he'll say when he sees us?'

'Hullo, there you are!' exclaimed Sally.

'My, how you've all grown! 'I suggested.

'Tsch!' said Pat.

'Well now, I guess you're hungry; but Mrs Jenks

has a champion tea waiting for you at High Tarn.'
This, of course, was Jan's suggestion.

'Certainly "Tsch!"' agreed Kay. 'And maybe any
of the others.'

'We'll soon know,' exclaimed Pat, 'because we're
there!'

Sure enough, the train – which had got up quite a
nice turn of speed on the last bit – was braking hard.
We scrambled for rukkers and gaberdines, and got
into quite a confused tangle. Mr Jenks must have
seen us at once, for we heard his voice booming away
from the dimness of the platform.

'Hullo, hullo!' he called. 'Well now, there you are.
Tsch, how you've all grown; I hardly knew you!
You'll be hungry, too; but there's a champion tea
waiting for you at High Tarn. Mrs Jenks has seen to
that.'

We tumbled out in a scrum, howling with laughter,
partly at our predictions being so right, partly just
from excitement. Then, quite suddenly, there we
were, all six of us (and I really believe it was Mr
Jenks who started it) linked together, and jigging and
leaping and whooping round in a giddy, whirling
ring.

The station-master stood still in amazement, pushed back his cap and scratched his head. I suppose he
thought that he was imagining things – unless, of
course, he too realized that he had seen us before.

'Now then, now then,' boomed Mr Jenks. 'This'll
never do. What about Mrs Jenks and the tea waiting
up at the farm. Are you forgetting them?'

'No!' I gasped, 'not forgetting; just being carried
away by our feelings!'

A giddy, whirling ring

'Come on, though,' said Pat. 'The trunks are still in the van. They'll be taking them back to London if we're not quick.'

'Noa,' said the jolly porter with the barrow. 'Noa, 'er waits 'ere a laal bit. Yer needna be in sech a 'urry, for 'er doan't go back Lunnon till maarnin'.'

We were in a hurry, though, and we set to work energetically to heave the trunks from the van on to a barrow, and then out to the farm lorry which Mr Jenks had parked at the side entrance. Pat took charge.

'Look out, Sally! Take the strain and heave-ho, my hearties! Hi, Jan, whoa! You're pushing too hard.'

'Aye, young Jan, you'll have the lorry and all over!' said Mr Jenks, bellowing with laughter. We could never understand why he found all we did so tremendously funny.

'Well now,' he said, as we got everything safely stowed between bags of meal, and spare wheels, and oddments of farm tackle. 'Into your usual places. The boys on the back, and the three lassies in the cab in front – if your legs haven't grown too long for all to get in.'

It was certainly a tight fit; but we're pretty good at doubling ourselves up, and tucking our legs away into odd spaces, and in no time we were grinding slowly down the steep slope in front of the station, and then getting up speed along the Ambleside road.

It was completely dark now, far too dark to see anything; but we knew it all so well, and could tell exactly where we were. As we swung up on to a rise a mile or two out of Windermere we saw, for the first time, the dim lights on the other side of the lake, shining from the farms and cottages below Claife Heights and round the edge of Pull Wyke. We glimpsed them again as we ran by the shore of the lake at Low Wood, and we knew that from here, by daylight, we should have had our first real view of all the high fells that encircle Coniston and the Langdale Valley – Dow Crags, the Old Man and Wetherlam, Crinkle Crags, Bowfell, and the Langdale Pikes themselves. We forked left to by-pass Ambleside.

'Waterhead,' I said; and then, a few minutes later, as we switchbacked violently, Kay gasped, 'Rothay Bridge!'

We ran fairly straight under the shoulder of Lough Rigg Fell, through Clappersgate, zigzagged up the Brathay Valley, then turned sharply left.

'Skelwith Bridge!' chirped Sally, before anyone-else could get it out.

'Right first time!' exclaimed Mr Jenks. 'You've not forgotten last summer, have you, young 'un?'

We were grinding uphill now, impatient of the slower speed, but glad to be climbing towards the fell farm. If we hadn't known that lorry we should never have believed it could do it. It groaned more horribly than the train had done on starting, but it went on, and on, and, slowly but surely, we got nearer. We forked left on to the little mountain road, and the jolts and bumps were terrific. But even though one of them made me bite my tongue quite painfully, I didn't mind. They were a sign that we were getting near.

Less than a hundred yards farther, with a sharp left turn, we swung through the gateway on to the track that leads up, through the fir copse and the rocky meadows to the farm itself.

Although the lorry didn't stop, Pat jumped off – it was the usual ritual – fastened the gate, and ran to catch up and leap on again. We bumped over the little hollow where the beck runs, chugged on again, crawled up the last steep pull before the farm gate, did a violent turn into the yard itself, jerked to a standstill – and were there. The light from indoors, streaming through the open doorway, dazzled us after the darkness we'd come through.

'Welcome back to High Tarn!' said Mr Jenks. 'And there's Mrs Jenks waiting to say it, too.'

We had the cab door open in a trice, and the boys were already scrambling off the back. But, somehow, Sally got ahead of all of us, and Mrs Jenks, despite her solidity, nearly went down under the young tornado that hurled itself at her. For half a minute she was completely winded, and her first welcome was just a tremendous smile. Then she managed to find breath to speak.

'Well now,' she gasped. 'If it isn't the best thing in the world to see you all again! But come along in; there's an extra special tea on the table, for you must all be starving, coming all the way from London without anything to eat – except, maybe, a few bits out of packets. Just run along and wash your hands as quick as you can. You'll feel a lot better, I dare say, when you've eaten something.'

And if we had had a game about it beforehand, we'd have guessed she would say exactly that.

CHAPTER 3

Old Friends Mostly

WE are always packed off to bed early on our first night in Westmorland, and this time, of course, it was dark before ever we got there. So, on the evening of our arrival, we didn't see any of our old friends except Mr and Mrs Jenks, and Raff and Betsy the sheepdogs.

But there was a new friend, too, in the kitchen, a very large, black cat – quite the biggest I've ever seen – curled up on top of the boiler at the side of the kitchen range. He stood up, stretched, and yawned as we came in, then jumped lazily down, strolled across to us, and threaded himself in and out of our legs. He seemed quite sure that we would like him.

'Ooh!' said Sally. 'He's new. Isn't he a pet! What's his name?'

'Mr Tiggle, we call him. Yes, he's new since you were last here. Walked in on us some time in October. No one'd ever seen him before, or knew where he'd come from; but he made himself at home at once, and he's a good mouser, so he earns his keep.'

'Mr Tiggle!' said Sally. 'What a lovely name. I think I'll have him for my special friend this holiday.'

Mr Tiggle absolutely boiled over with purrs, so he must have liked the idea, and he followed Sally around more closely than her own shadow till early bedtime.

Jan and I always used to think up the most terrific expeditions to begin the very first morning. It seemed such a waste of time not to get into the thick of things at once. But they never came off. Mrs Jenks says that we need to get over the journey, and she insists on us being in for all meals very punctually on the first day, so that she is sure that we are not wandering too far. Mrs Jenks doesn't have many rules, fewer than most grown-ups, I should think; but the ones she has, she has very thoroughly.

This time we began as usual after breakfast by going to see Bobbin the cart-horse. He and Raff, who came bounding along at our heels, are our oldest friends among the animals, and always expect to be greeted first.

Bobbin was in his stall, having his breakfast of oats and hay. He enjoys his meals, and likes to be left to munch his way steadily through them. So it must have meant that he was glad to see us when he lifted his head out of the manger, and whinnied, and snuffled his nostrils. He remembered us all quite well, I'm sure. For one thing he muzzled into my hand for the lump of sugar I usually brought him. Luckily I'd remembered, too.

We left him after a time, because it seemed only fair to let him get on with his breakfast; and, besides, there were other visits to make. Mr Jenks was busy milking, an after-breakfast job in winter. We went into the byre to say good morning to the cows, and to pick out the ones we knew.

'Here's the big, red one,' I said. 'The one with the stocky legs, and the specially turned-up nose.'

'And here's the one with the right horn pointing forwards, and the left horn back. Gives her such an astonished look, doesn't it?'

'Mm! She was my favourite last summer.'

'Oh, here's the one without any horns at all.'

'Those two in the end stalls are new, aren't they?'

'Aye. Had them about a month,' said Mr Jenks.

'They're shorthorns, aren't they?'

'Northern dairy shorthorns; best for these fell farms.'

High Tarn is mainly, of course, a sheep farm. There are never more than about a dozen cows; but Mr Jenks is always proud of their condition.

We moved on again, this time to the pigsty. Here we found another old friend, Louisa the huge, white sow. She was lying in a patch of winter sunshine, on one fat white side, looking like a pale, inflated airship. She didn't move, of course, but she gave a little grunt, and winked one little, black eye very solemnly.

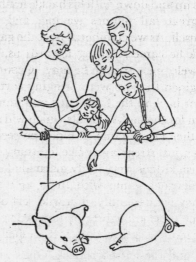

Winked one little, black eye

This was really quite a warm greeting from Louisa, who doesn't put herself out for anyone.

'Don't believe she'd do more if the Queen called to see her,' said Kay.

There were two young pigs in the other sty. They were a lot more active, and came across to us, grunting and snuffling. We hadn't met them before, but we made friends at once. Pat scratched them just behind their ears, and they stood with little piggy eyes tight shut, and expressions of utter bliss on their faces. Sally laughed so hard that she had a choking fit, and had to be thumped on the back vigorously.

The fowl-houses are in the little intak, just beyond the farm-yard, and we went over there next. We don't know the hens individually, they are all so much alike – and just a bit dull. But there is one huge cock that struts up and down with his hackle feathers puffed and his great tail plumes waving, and thinks no end of himself. As we clambered over the gate into the little intak he came strutting towards us, which we took as a welcome – though he may, of course, simply have imagined that we were bringing corn.

We went back to the farm-yard and hunted about in the barn for the half-wild cats which will sometimes play a rather fierce game of hide-and-seek, and, at other times, just streak away like lightning. We found two smallish kittens, very fluffy marmalades, and had quite a hilarious game with them and a piece of string. They were friendly, in a wild sort of way, but never came close enough to be touched; and, in the end, their mother, a thin, dark tortoiseshell, darted in and hustled them away.

'What time is it, Kay?' asked Pat at this point.

'My goodness! Twenty-nine and a half minutes past twelve. Half a minute to dinner. Come on!'

We streaked out of the barn almost as quickly as the cats had done, and just about managed to make it without any rules broken.

'What plans for this afternoon?' I asked, as we sat round the table feeling very well fed after our first High Tarn dinner.

'Baking for me,' said Sally. She is convinced that that job can't be managed without her. I believe she must imagine that Mr and Mrs Jenks hibernate during term time.

'Let's go down to Skelwith to see the Wetherbys,' suggested Kay.

Farmer and Mrs Wetherby are old friends. It isn't more than two miles or so each way to Plover Rigg, their farm near Skelwith Bridge, so we could fit it quite easily into the afternoon, and be back punctually for tea.

As we tramped down the path through the rocky meadows to the high road, we got our first real view of the high fells. They couldn't have looked more perfect, the whole round of them, Wetherlam, Crinkles, Bowfell and the Langdale Pikes, white-capped with snow, reddish brown with dead bracken below, and absolutely bathed in winter sunshine that somehow, on distant things, looks even warmer than summer.

It was great fun to come upon so many old friends on the way. We met the postman, toiling up one of the steep brows, with head well down and pushing a laden bicycle. He looked up as we drew near, then grinned broadly.

'Ee well!' he exclaimed as he mopped his face. 'So yer back agin at 'Igh Tarn. An' 'oo is t'a all?'

Mr Jenks, years ago, taught us the right answer to that one, so we were able to give it correctly in broad dialect.

'*Ee, thanks, wur champion!*'

'Ee, thanks, wur champion!' we said in chorus.

'An' t'other yan, t'laal lassie; 'ave yer not fetched 'er wi' yer?'

'Oh yes,' said Kay. 'Sally's busy helping Mrs Jenks to bake. And she's champion, too.'

We must have answered the same question half a dozen times before we got back, for we met old Mrs Thwaites from Beck Cottage, and Jem Longmire the shepherd from Becker Brow, and Farmer Benson, and a road mender, and one or two others.

We had our usual warm welcome from Farmer and

Mrs Wetherby at Plover Rigg. We saw the colt that had been a tiny foal last time we were there, and Star's litter of sheep-dog puppies, just at the playful scrapping stage. We heard the good news that Bill Wetherby, who farms now on the far side of Skiddaw, would be home for Christmas; and, before we dashed off to be in time for tea, we promised to come down again soon.

As a matter of fact we were home early, and Jan and I had time to go to the byre to talk to Mr Jenks who was just finishing afternoon milking. Jan wanted to ask about some of the birds that he'd known in summer, especially about Barny, the big owl, who lived away behind the rafters in the barn.

'Aye,' said Farmer Jenks. 'He's still there – looking wiser than ever. I've seen him sometimes at dusk, and once or twice early in the morning, gliding between the barn and the ash tree, like a big, pale moth you might think. And many a time I've heard him hooting at night. Off on his hunting, no doubt.'

Mr Jenks had also seen a kingfisher down at Brathay Bridge, a raven on the wooded crags beside Tarn Hows, and dippers along the beck. Jan said that he must go off bird-watching as soon as he got the chance.

We helped to carry the milk pails from the byre, and stopped by the gate to look over towards the fells which were now only black shapes against what was left of the sunset. The rest of the sky was just beginning to fade into darkness, and the first star had come out.

'Looks good, doesn't it?' I said.

'Aye,' agreed Farmer Jenks, who knows all the

weather signs. 'And set for a long, fine spell, I think.'

You can guess that the others were pleased when we told them this at tea-time. It seemed the best possible beginning to a winter holiday.

CHAPTER 4

Tally-Ho!

'GOLLY!' exclaimed Jan. 'It's a stunning morning. I could run a mile!'

'Five!'

'Ten!'

'Twenty!' I suggested recklessly, joining the others at the door. 'What are we going to do about it?'

We all considered the question.

'I know!' said Pat with sudden inspiration. 'What about hares and hounds?'

'You mean – a sort of paper chase?'

'Yes; only without the paper.'

'How do we follow, then? No use dragging aniseed as they do for a real hound trail; we'd never smell it.'

'Oh, hares leave signs and messages. Better than dropping litter all over the place.'

'Do we have one hare and three hounds, or two and two?'

'Two and two's better.'

'How'll we divide?' I asked.

'You and Pat one set, Jan and me the other,' suggested Kay.

'Right,' I agreed. 'Do we toss for hares?'

'I think it'd better be you and Pat this time, because he's done it before.'

'There's Sally, too, of course,' said Pat a bit dubiously. The infant was just coming across the farmyard with a basin of scraps in her arms, and Mr Tiggle hard on her heels.

'I say, Sally,' called Kay, 'Are you awfully busy today?'

'Ooh, yes!' said Sally. 'I'm just going to feed the chicks, and I've promised to take some eggs down to Mrs Thwaites, and I expect that I'll be helping to bake.'

Mr Tiggle hard on her heels

'We're doing a sort of hares and hounds chase. Like to come?'

'We-ll, I don't think I'd better,' said Sally, obviously feeling her importance as the one member of the family with work to do. 'Mrs Jenks might not be able to manage without me.'

She and Mr Tiggle went on with the chicken scraps into the little intak.

'That's all right then,' said Pat. Of course we would have taken Sally if she had wanted to come, but we would have had to cut down the route a bit.

'Look here,' suggested Kay. 'Suppose Jan and I deal with the lunches while you two get ready; then you can be away as soon as possible. How much start do we have to give you?'

'Quarter of an hour, not more. Ten minutes might be enough.'

'Make it fifteen. Don't want to catch up too soon,' said Jan with his usual optimism.

So Kay and Jan went off to see Mrs Jenks about sandwich fillings, while Pat and I dashed to get ready for the chase.

'Rubbers for speed, or nails for rough going?' I called to him, as I sat on the bedroom floor, pulling on thick socks.

'Rubbers, I think, don't you? May get a bit muddy, but speed's the main thing today. By the way, have you got a pencil? We'll need to leave messages.'

'Yes, here's one; paper too. I'll put them in my haversack. Anything else?'

'Bit of chalk might be useful, if you've got any.'

'There's a stick in my pencil box; bright pink. By the way, where do we start from?'

'Right here. We'll tell them to look for the first clue in the front porch, and we'll leave a note there to direct them.'

'Where'll we send them from there?'

'Somewhere quite straight-forward to begin, I think. Let's just tell them to go down the cart track through the meadows to the gate, and to look for the next clue there. If you're quite ready would you like to write that on a bit of paper, and put it in the porch – under the bench, or somewhere out of sight?'

'Right-ho!' I agreed. Then I had an idea. 'I say, Pat, how about writing the clues in poetry?'

'My hat! What a notion! Don't you think it would hold us up too much, racking our brains for rhymes and things?'

'Gracious, no! We can easily rattle off a bit of dog-gerel,' I said – rather airily, I suppose. 'I'll get going at once.'

So I sat on the bedroom floor, scribbling down the first poetic fragment, while Pat collected the rest of his things together.

'This do?' I whispered, as he came across the landing.

> 'Down meadow path the hares have fled.
>   (The hunt is up, sing view halloo!)
> The farm gate on the mountain road
>   Will offer you the second clue.'

'Right enough,' said Pat with a grin. 'But I bet Jan'll have a fit when he finds his instructions dished up in a sonnet!'

'Well, not a sonnet quite: I think a sonnet has something a bit special about it.'

'Never mind, it'll do. Don't let them see you hide it, will you?'

Kay and Jan had finished in the kitchen, and came dashing upstairs at this moment; so the coast was clear. I crept down quietly, and slipped the paper under the door-mat in the front porch. We took a peep into the lunch packets as we stowed them away.

They looked heartening, two sorts of sandwiches, two slices of rich fruit cake, and half a dozen biscuits per head.

'Sure you've got everything?' asked Pat. 'Pencil, paper, chalk – ?'

'I think so. We'd better get going, hadn't we? The others'll be ready soon.'

We could hear them upstairs, scrambling round after their things – particularly Jan, whose possessions are always a bit scattered.

'Hi, you two!' called Pat. 'Is everything clear? You give us fifteen minutes start, and then follow. It's just thirteen – no fourteen minutes past ten by the grandfather clock. That means that you set out at ten-twenty-nine exactly; and you'll find your first clue in the porch. O.K.? Come on, then, Hyacinth. G'bye, Sally. We're awa-a-y!'

'Good hunting!' yelled Sally excitedly, waving her wooden spoon, and scattering cake mixture recklessly.

'Tally-ho!' I called (though I believe I should have left that one for the hunters), and shot after Pat across the farm-yard.

CHAPTER 5

View Halloo!

WE went through the meadows like the wind.
The ground was icy hard; we'd rubbers on our feet;
and, of course, the cart track is gloriously steep. In
what seemed like seconds we were at the gate leading
out on to the mountain road that goes up from Oxenfell past Tarn Hows.

'Now, I suppose, we leave the next instructions?'
I said.

'Yes, but it doesn't need a note. It's only a question of whether they turn right or left.'

'Mightn't they think we'd gone straight over the
opposite wall?'

'No, not unless we'd left very clear indications that
we'd done so. It isn't a path, you see.'

'Then all we need to do is to put a little arrow to
show we've turned left – I suppose we *are* heading for
the tarn?'

'Mm! Could do it that way; but I think it would be
a better idea to block the other direction.'

'How?'

'Like this,' said Pat, gathering up some rounded
stones between egg and orange size, and arranging
them across the road to the right of the gate. I set to
work, too, and in half a minute we'd got a row of
them stretching right across, not *too* obviously; in
fact you might have missed them, easily, but you
would certainly have noticed them in the end if you
were really looking for an indication. Then we turned
left, and ran off that way up the road.

I set to work, too

The next halt came where the ladder over the wall leads off to the tarn. It's only about half a mile on, but I can tell you that I was panting long before then, from the steepness of the road.

'Where – do – we – go – from – here?' I gasped, taking a deep gulp between each word.

'Over the ladder and along the path to Tom Ghyll, don't you think?'

'Then – we – block – off the road ahead, I suppose?'

'Well, we blocked last time. Let's mark the way this. Do it with your chalk, it doesn't need much; just a sort of little arrow, and "On to Tom Ghyll".'

'It's a frightful pink colour. Won't it be awfully obvious?'

'Do it somewhere a bit out of sight. They'll know there's a choice of routes here, because this is a definite path; so they'll search for some sign.'

So I wrote it on the wall underneath one of the wooden steps of the ladder, and, because it did look rather awful to leave chalk marks about, I added instructions below:

ON TO TOM GHYLL
(Please rub out)

We scrambled over and dashed along the rough path, through the dead bracken and between the fir trees, to the edge of the tarn, and round to the spot where the ghyll flows out and goes leaping off down Glen Mary. Here Pat suggested a bold plan.

'I say, Hyacinth, let's lead them off down the glen right to the very bottom.'

'The old saw-mill, and Yew Tree Farm?'

'Mm! Then make them double back on their tracks till they come to the path that goes to the right about half-way up, and lead them off along that.'

'Fine! I can see Jan looking wild when he gets down there and then discovers he's to come back again.'

'We'll have to cache a note for them here, directing them down to Yew Tree Farm,' said Pat.

So I sat down and scribbled off my next bit of doggerel, while Pat collected pebbles and arranged them just on the edge of the little stone viaduct to read:

STOP! LOOK!

My verse said:

> To reach the gate of Yew Tree Farm,
> If asked the way, the guide would tell

'Follow Tom Ghyll down Mary Glen.'
That way pursue the hares, as well.

We cached it under a large stone at the edge of the water, then raced off down the glen. I was beginning to get into the swing of it, and enjoy it all tremendously. But as we leapt, and slithered, and scrambled down the steep, rocky track, a rather annoying idea crossed my mind.

'Look here, Pat. Isn't this a bit risky? Suppose on *their* way down they find the clue we leave, on *our* way back, where the path leads off. They'd short-circuit and probably catch us up.'

'Oh, I don't think so. The last note tells them to go right on to Yew Tree Farm, doesn't it? So they won't be looking for a clue again before then. If we hide the half-way one fairly well they'll never notice it. The biggest risk for us will be that they'll be pretty close as we come back, and may see us.'

'Mm! And all this stopping to leave clues delays us a bit.'

'Yes. But they're delayed by stopping to find them.'

'Here's the path we're going to switch them on to when they come back. I say, Pat, would it save time if I wrote the next clue at once – the one we're leaving at Yew Tree Farm – and you hared down with it to hide it, while I stayed here to write the next one – the one we're going to leave here?'

'Good idea!' grinned Pat. 'It'll give you time to polish up the poetry.'

I sat down on a stone, thought for a few seconds, then scribbled down my third bit of doggerel.

'Here it is:

'Too fast, too far, the hounds have run.
(They win the chase who travel less,
Ah flying, reckless, heedless feet,
That cover ground, but don't progress.)
So now they must retrace their steps,
Climb half-way back, and then digress.'

'Good!' said Pat. 'I think you probably hold the speed record for poetry!'

I handed it over. 'Leave it by the gate-post, or as near as you can. I'll sit here and get on with the next.'

'Better not sit *here*, had you, in case they're hard on our heels, and catch up to you before I get back. Look, go and hide yourself behind those shrubs where the rocks overhang. You'll be quite out of sight there.'

'O.K. Looks a bit dampish, but I don't suppose you'll be long. You'll have to take care coming back, won't you? They'll surely be somewhere about by then.'

'Mm! I'll skirt around a bit through the trees. I don't think I need to come by the actual path, except where it crosses the ghyll.'

I settled down in my dampish hide-out, and Pat went haring off. You can get up a pretty speed in rubbers over steep, rocky slopes like this – though it does look rather perilous to life and limb; so I knew that he would be back very soon.

He was. I suddenly saw him mounting quietly through the woods rather over to the south of the path. I'd only just finished my next verse, certainly not had time for any polish. He didn't speak until he was right up to me. We were in the danger zone, now, and had to take all precautions.

'Is the deathless verse ready?' he whispered.

'Ready,' I said, 'but not deathless. It's a putrid rhyme.'

'Doesn't matter so long as the instructions are clear. What does it say, and where does it go?'

'It says:

> 'If you had counted rather less
> On speed, but used your eyes instead,
> You might have spied hares lurking here;
> And so cut out the herring red.
>
> This by-pass to the view-point leads.
> Pray waste no time upon the view
> But press on to the further gate.
> Then look about ere passing through.'

'Put it underneath that boulder, the one bang in the middle of the path. Screw it up a bit, so that it's hidden.'

Pat crept over to the track and cached the note. Just as he got it there I saw him stiffen up suddenly, listening. Then, swiftly and silently as a panther, he slid back to the hide-out.

'What is it?' I whispered. 'Are they near?'

'Ssh!'

We crouched there with ears stretched, listening intently. A twig cracked somewhere above, then another. There was certainly someone about.

The noises got louder and louder, and suddenly,

like a young tornado, there was Jan coming helter-
skelter down the path, with Kay absolutely at his
heels. They leapt in turn on to the boulder, and I
nearly had a heart attack, thinking that it would turn
over and that they'd find the note. But it didn't. They

Kay absolutely at his heels

went on, dashing at top speed, set on getting to Yew
Tree Farm as quickly as possible.

'Well!' I gasped weakly, as soon as they'd disappeared down. 'That *was* a narrow shave.'

'*And* they're jolly close! Come on, Hyacinth; we'd
better get up speed, too. This one directs them to the
gate across the road, about a quarter of a mile beyond
the view-point, doesn't it? Right! Full speed ahead
to there, then. Let's hope they're held up a bit trying
to find the two notes.'

That was certainly a narrow shave – though not, in fact, as narrow as the one that came right at the end. But the whole chase was tremendous fun. We never got over the feeling that the others were just on our heels, and we didn't dare slack off at all. We even ate lunch on the run, just about twelve-thirty, as near as we could judge from the sun.

'I s'pose this is what you'd call a running buffet,' said Pat, munching and cantering at the same time.

'Mm!' I panted. 'And I don't think it's the best thing for digestion. I don't remember *ever* leaving anything before, but I can't possibly eat this second piece of cake. I s'pose you wouldn't like it?'

'No thanks. I feel a bit stuffed myself.'

'Mine's like a hard lump – just there. I thought it'd be lighter to carry when it was inside; but it isn't. What shall I do with this cake?'

'Leave it with the next note for Jan. I don't mind betting he'll manage it, and it may hold them up a bit.'

'Good idea! It's rather soggy, 'cos I dropped it into the ghyll; but I dare say it'll have dried out by that time, or frozen hard.'

So, when we got to the spot where the field path from Hawkshead Hill to Hawkshead crosses the beck by a little bridge, I took out a bigger piece of paper and wrote my verse on that. I didn't take long; I'd been turning it over in my mind as I ran, and I scribbled it down at once.

Colthouse Farm gate the next direction.
(We hope you will not raise objection.)

And – so to help you in the running –
This fruit cake may prove rather stunning.
But, may we make a wise suggestion?
You pause a while, to aid digestion.

'I think the bit about digestion's rather good,' I said, as I wrapped the paper round the cake, and cached them on a stone just above water level.

'Don't suppose Jan knows the meaning of the word,' said Pat with a grin. 'Still, it may slow them down for a minute or two, and that'll be all to the good.'

We did a fine round. From the tarn we had come down by Borwick Lodge and Hawkshead Hill, and along the field path to Hawkshead. Then we went on along the Sawrey road, but only as far as Colthouse, where we cut on to Claife Heights, past the trout hatcheries to the plantations. There we did a sharp left turn, and scrambled downhill to Far Wray. We found a path round by Blelham Tarn – a rather unpleasantly soggy one, I must admit – to Outgate. From Outgate we headed for Barngate, cut into the woods nearby, scrambled up on to Black Fell, and over the great, rugged top towards High Tarn.

And all the way, of course, we were leaving signs and clues, blocking paths with lines or stones, and showing directions with arrows – chalked, or scratched in the dust, or made from twigs – and writing notes. I must have turned out some yards of poetry.

It was just as well that this meant an occasional halt, because apart from these we never let up all day, and it was jolly strenuous going. There were things we'd have liked to linger over. We saw what we

C

thought were coot on Blelham; and the people from the freshwater biological station were doing something jolly interesting in the mud of a tarn they'd drained on Claife Heights. But we didn't dare to stop unnecessarily. We were so sure that Kay and Jan must be almost on our heels.

We never actually did see them again till the end, and when at last we jogged on to the rocky outcrop just above High Tarn we felt sure that we'd made it. They couldn't possibly catch us now.

'I say,' suggested Pat. 'Let's not go on yet. Let's wait till they're almost up to us, and give them a last run for their money.'

'Oh, lovely!' I agreed. 'It'll be fun to have a really spectacular finish.'

We dropped down on to the rock, quite glad to cool off. But that wasn't difficult. It was late afternoon, and, though the sun hadn't really gone down, there was an absolutely icy grip in the air. We didn't have to wait long.

'Hullo!' exclaimed Pat, suddenly. 'I think I can see them.'

We strained our eyes. Sure enough, there they were, jogging along among the outcrop rocks some distance away.

'We'll stand up when they're fairly close,' chuckled Pat, 'and whistle to them.'

We did; and I suppose we must have looked quite startling, standing black against the sunset. They stopped for a moment in amazement, then came on towards us with a last, tremendous spurt.

'Yoicks!' yelled Pat, and 'Tally-ho!' I added. Then we leapt off the rock and dived for home.

We had got a good start still, so had no real fears of being overtaken. But, of course, the unexpected sometimes happens – and it did today.

Pat was already half-way across the farm-yard, and I a few feet behind. I suppose my plaits were flying about madly, and suddenly, as I dived under the tree

'Help, Pat, help!'

by the gate, I felt myself caught as if in a vice – fastened, in fact, by the hair to one of the low boughs.

'Help, Pat, help!' I shrieked. 'I'm stuck! Save me!'

Pat, seeing what had happened, doubled back; and there followed the most unpleasant thirty seconds of my life. It seemed like thirty minutes.

Pat tugged and pulled, and I wriggled and jerked, but couldn't get free. I could hear their footsteps pounding closer and closer, and Pat muttering what sounded like the most frightful nautical oaths between his clenched teeth. Mr Tiggle watched with calm interest from his favourite perch on the pigsty roof. I could just see him through the corner of my eye.

'Pull harder,' I said, nearly sobbing with pain. 'Hard as you can!'

'I *am* doing. I s'pose you haven't got any scissors with you?'

At that moment, with a sickening wrench, I came free, and I swear that there's a bald patch to this day at the back of my head – if only I could see it.

It was none too soon. Pat flew for the porch; I followed; and a hair's breadth behind came Kay and Jan. We each made a superhuman dive over the last yard, and finished in a tangled heap on the door-mat.

Mr Tiggle jumped down from the pigsty roof and came carefully across the farm-yard to take a look. I don't suppose that he will ever again see a closer finish to a paper chase.

CHAPTER 6

Sleuthing Jan

I HAD had my suspicions of Jan for two days. He had been behaving in such a fishy way, and I was amazed that the others didn't seem to have noticed.

It was the way he kept disappearing, twice a day usually, just after breakfast first, and then again in the afternoon. I never actually saw him go; but, sudden-

Looking remarkably innocent

ly, he just wasn't with us any longer – nor anywhere about, however hard you searched. Then, some time later he would come sauntering in, looking remarkably innocent – which, in Jan, is a sure sign of guilt.

I didn't say anything to the others, but I decided that I'd do a bit of sleuthing on my own, and see if I couldn't get to the bottom of it.

I tried first of all in the morning, and concentrated so hard on keeping him in view that I nearly burst myself in the attempt. I did, in fact, break a saucer as I helped with the washing-up – mainly because I tried to keep my eyes on the window to see whether he went past. Pat said, rather crossly, that I wasn't giving my full attention to the matter in hand. He was *quite* right.

But Jan was still there when I'd finished. He seemed to be collecting things together, but I couldn't make out what. He did it in so much quieter a way than usual. So I flapped around doing a few rather unnecessary jobs of my own, and trying to keep him in the corner of my eye.

Then, quite suddenly, he had gone. He must have slipped through the front door while I was putting the domino box away at the back of the cupboard in the dresser. When I pulled my head out of the depths, there just wasn't a sign of him. I waited for about thirty seconds; then I, too, slipped through the front door.

He was nowhere in sight, not even when I scrambled to the top of the rocky knoll. That meant that he couldn't have gone down the cart track through the meadows, nor to the left up the fells. He wouldn't have had time to get out of sight either way. So he must have turned right, gone across the little intak, over the wall at the far end, and into the fir trees where the fellside slopes down steeply. That way brings you eventually to the mountain road. I went after him as speedily as I could, with my eyes wide open for any signs.

But there just weren't any. By the time I'd crossed

the intak and scrambled over the far wall, he seemed to have disappeared completely from the face of the earth. There wasn't so much as a glimpse of his blue sweater through the trees.

I went on by what seemed the likeliest track, down through the fir copse, over some rocky bits of fellside, and out, in the end, on to the Tarn Hows mountain road. But it is such a rugged region, with clumps of firs and rocky knolls, that he might quite easily have been not very far away without my knowing.

I gave it up in the end, and scrambled back through the fir copse to High Tarn. Jan came sauntering in about twenty minutes later, looking altogether too innocent, and making some remark about the sheep in the meadows just below. I didn't say anything, but I determined that I wouldn't be beaten next time.

We had no special plans for the day; so, as soon as dinner was over, I went upstairs, gathered together my lamb's-wool mitts, a woolly scarf, and an extra thick pullover – a plain, neutral shade, so that I could fade quite nicely into the background. Then I slipped out of the house, through the farm-yard and the little intak, scrambled over the wall at the far end, and searched about for a hiding-place.

There was a good one about a hundred yards away, a sort of nook where the wall twisted. I crept into it and sat down on a stone. I felt beautifully hidden, though I could see everything.

It was a brilliant afternoon, absolutely sparkling, but icy cold despite the sunshine and the mitts and things. I sat there watching, completely still, and getting more and more frigid. But this time I was determined to succeed, even if I perished in the attempt.

And luck was with me. After about half an hour I saw Jan scramble over the wall from the intak, and slip into the fir copse and down the fellside. I forgot all about my stiffness and coldness, and was after him like a shot.

He went on at a great rate, through the firs and across the rough, rocky little meadows below, and I went after him. I didn't want to catch up until I'd

Sat there watching

discovered where he was going, so I tried to keep one wall between us all the time. I would watch from behind one until I'd seen him climb over the next. Then I would scramble over mine and hare across the meadow to the one he'd just gone over. And, in the end, the plan worked. As I peered over a wall I saw that he had perched himself on top of the next, and was staring hard ahead. It was the wall, I realized, at the edge of the little tarn – the one that isn't marked on any of the ordnance maps.

I skimmed across the rocky ground between us as silently as I could. He seemed to be concentrating tremendously on something just ahead, and I got right up to him before I spoke.

'So *this* is where you are!' I said suddenly.

Jan swung round in astonishment.

'Hyacinth!' he exclaimed. 'However did *you* get here?'

'Sleuthed you,' I said, 'all the way from the farm.'

'Blow!'

'It's no use blowing; I've had my suspicions for days. You'd better come clean,' I told him grimly.

I thought, for a moment, that Jan was going to be simply furious. Then suddenly he grinned – his usual, cheery grin.

'Might have known I couldn't keep it dark from you' he admitted.

'Of course you might,' I said, scrambling up on the wall beside him. 'But whatever is "it", and why did you want to keep it dark?'

'Ssh!' said Jan – a most unusual remark from him. 'And do be careful you don't sit on those things.'

'Whatever on earth – !' I exclaimed, noticing the 'things' for the first time.

There was a sardine tin, opened very jaggedly – with a pen-knife, I suppose, and half full of a smushy mess of sardines. Beside it was a piece of grease-proof paper, overflowing with bacon rinds and crumbs and crusts of bread.

'Gracious! You're not having a solitary picnic, are you?'

'No, of course not. They're for Old Nod.'

'Old Nod?'

'Mm! I've been bringing him things to eat, twice a day.'

'Yes. I watched you disappear regularly. That's why I sleuthed you.'

'Trust you,' grinned Jan.

'Look,' I said, feeling that this conversation was going round in circles and not really getting anywhere. 'Couldn't you begin the story at the beginning, go straight on, and finish at the end? That's what I'm trying to do with the Blood-stained Hippopotamus; it's the best way, I find, in the long run.'

'All right,' agreed Jan. 'But you *will* keep on asking questions and interrupting.'

'I'll be silent as the grave, once you've started!' I promised.

CHAPTER 7

Old Nod

'IT began,' Jan said, 'three days ago, just as the frost came. I was coming back from Tarn Hows this way because several times I'd seen a heron fishing close to the edge of the water, and I could watch quite easily from behind this wall.

'This time he was there as usual, standing absolutely still except when he made a sudden dart at a fish. I saw him catch one and come up with it crossways in his bill. Then he gave a great swallow, and it went down his throat whole.'

'Goodness!' I exclaimed, forgetting about the grave that I was to be silent as. 'How indigestible!'

'I hoped I'd see him bag another,' continued Jan. 'So I crouched by the wall for a bit. But he didn't have any luck, and it really was getting frigidly cold. I could feel everything beginning to stiffen, and I thought there was a sort of skim of ice forming on the water. But he just stood there, not seeming to notice the cold.'

'Huh!' I shivered, remembering my own cold and solitary watch by the wall that afternoon.

'Well, I couldn't stay for very long. My teeth were beginning to chatter, and anyhow I knew that it was just on tea-time, and I'd have to run like anything to be there in time.'

'I can quite understand that you wouldn't want to miss that,' I said.

'Of *course* not! For one thing I knew there'd be crumpets. But I couldn't stop thinking about that heron. I'd read about the way they would sometimes stand in the water till it froze hard all round them, and fastened them in; and if it went on long enough they'd die from hunger and cold.'

'Seems an awfully silly thing to do, doesn't it?' I remarked.

'Yes, but I knew it was true because I've read about it several times. And I couldn't forget the way this fellow had stood there, absolutely still, while the skin formed on the water, and the air got colder and colder. I even woke in the night and thought about it.'

'It *must* have been on your mind!'

'It was, and next morning I decided that I'd hare down to the tarn as soon as ever I got a chance. I went the moment we'd finished washing the breakfast things.'

'Good of you to stay to help with those!' I said.

'Not really,' grinned Jan. 'Just common sense. I knew there'd have been a hullabaloo if I'd cut, and I didn't want anyone to notice.'

'I see. And the heron was still there, I suppose?'

'Yes,' said Jan. 'But who's telling this story?'

'Sorry,' I said. 'You are. Do please go on; it's getting quite exciting.'

'Well, I came down about half past nine. The tarn was frozen iron hard, and there, in just the same spot, was Old Nod, standing stiff as a board, with his one leg clamped in the ice, and his other tucked away, just as it had been the night before.'

'Poor thing! Was he still alive?'

'I couldn't tell; he might just have been frozen stiff. So I crept out over the ice. He was only about six feet from the edge, and in quite shallow water, of course, so there wasn't any danger even if it broke, and I guessed that it wouldn't do that, because it felt firm as dry land. When I got to him and touched him I knew he was still alive, because he gave a sort of quiver; but he couldn't move any more than that. I saw that I'd have to smash the ice to get his leg out, and I was afraid that I'd find then that it had been broken.'

'Poor thing!' I said again.

'I dashed back to the edge,' Jan went on, 'and got the biggest stone I could use. Then I crept out again to him, and started to smash the ice all round. It was a beastly job, because it was frozen so hard and thick that it took an awful lot of breaking. But I didn't want to frighten him more than I could help, or hurt his leg, either. I got it smashed up in the end and as his leg came free he just flopped on to the surface and lay there.'

'Poor thing!' I said for the third time. 'Did he die?'

'No, but he was so weak that he couldn't move, except for a sort of quiver when I touched him. So I just picked him up – he seemed *huge* close to – and carried him as carefully as I could to the side. Then I put him down and had a look at his leg.'

'Was it broken?'

'I didn't think so; it seemed quite straight. I was jolly thankful, because I don't know what I'd have done then. I might have tried to set it with a sliver of wood, and my hankie for a bandage.'

'You'd have been lucky to find that you had one with you – unless Kay'd reminded you that morning!'

'Stop interrupting!' said Jan. 'Anyhow I thought it wasn't broken, which was a jolly good thing because it would probably never have come really right again; and birds are so helpless once they've been damaged, and can't live in the ordinary way. They generally die soon, from hunger or something. But it was bruised and stiff and swollen, and Old Nod was too weak to move or do anything.'

'Stop interrupting!'

'What did you do?'

'First of all I found a nice, sheltered hollow among the roots of a tree, and I tore up masses of dead bracken and dry grass for a bed. Then I carried him over and put him down as comfortably as I could, with bracken all round and over him.'

'Wouldn't he need food, too?'

'Yes, so as soon as I'd got him settled I dashed off to High Tarn to scavenge some scraps.'

'And you've been feeding him ever since?'

'Mm! And it hasn't been easy, I can tell you.'

'What does he eat?'

'Well, normally fish, and little frogs and newts and things.'

'You wouldn't be able to catch fish for him with the tarn still frozen hard.'

'No. I might have got him a frog or two, but it seemed so hard on them, and anyhow he was too weak at first to deal with anything so lively as a frog.'

'Mm! I see that. What did you give him?'

'Well, I scavenged all the bacon rinds I could lay hands on, and crusts of bread and things.'

'The crusts must have been hard to come by,' I said. (We're a great crust-eating family.)

'They were. I managed a few by bagging them for myself, and then not eating them.'

'Jolly noble of you!'

'Yes, I thought so too; but it was awfully hard to get enough, because birds eat a tremendous lot, you know. Yesterday when I went into Ambleside with Mr Jenks I bought a tin of sardines. That's it you're sitting on now.'

'No, I'm not quite,' I said. But I was greatly impressed. Jan is usually pretty nearly penniless, and it must have taken his last farthing. 'And how is he getting on now?'

'Marvellously!' said Jan. 'Yesterday afternoon, when I came down, he was standing on both legs, and tottering about a bit.'

'Doesn't he mind your going close?'

'No. He seems to have got used to me when he was absolutely helpless and couldn't move away. I suppose he connects me with meal-times now.'

'You haven't fed him yet this afternoon?'

'No. It's time I did. I was just going down to him when you came sleuthing along.'

'I suppose he'd mind if I came too?' I said, rather sadly.

'I think so, probably,' said Jan. 'But look. If you creep round to the back of that tree – d'you see which I mean, the sycamore with the broken bough? – I think you'd have a good view.'

'O.K.,' I agreed, sliding off the wall. 'I'll try to move as quietly as I did when I was sleuthing you!'

Jan grinned, gathered up the food from the wall, and went on down the path. He moved, not actually silently, but quietly and fairly slowly; and he whistled softly, I suppose to give Old Nod warning that he was coming. I crept to the back of the sycamore and watched. And I wouldn't have missed doing that for anything.

The heron, a grey and white bird, and huge when seen so close, was standing quite motionless by the bed of bracken in the bole of the tree. As it heard the sound of whistling it turned its wedge-shaped head, with the long, strong, pointed bill, and watched Jan approach. It seemed completely fearless of him.

Jan didn't go right up to it, but stopped short about three yards away, and spread the food on the ground. Then he moved back a bit and the heron stepped stiffly forward.

I can tell you that it enjoyed that meal! The bacon rinds went down in three gulps, (I expect that it thought they were worms, or eels or something); the crusts, broken up and smeared with sardine paste, followed; and it finished off with the two whole sardines that you could still see were fish. The second of these it held sideways through its beak for a moment, then tossed it in the air, caught it, and swallowed it whole. I expect it was pretending that it was its own catch.

I was tremendously grateful to Jan for telling me everything and letting me watch.

'It was awfully decent of you to come clean about it,' I said, as we went back through the fir copse.

'Oh, that's all right,' said Jan. 'You'll be able to help to scavenge food tomorrow and bring it down with me.'

'Ooh! May I really?' I said.

I can tell you that I worked hard at the job and, by the time we were free to slip away next morning, we'd got a wonderful pile – crusts (two people's offerings this time), bacon rinds, sausage scraps, and some kipper skins. I even brought a bagful of fish meal from the barn. It certainly *smelt* fishy enough.

'I wonder how much longer it will go on depending on us for food,' I said as we scrambled down through the firs.

'Not long, I think. It seemed so much stronger yesterday – almost normal in fact. I do hope that it gets really right so that it can live a proper life again.'

'It'll be sad to lose it, won't it?'

'Mm, in a way; but you wouldn't want a bird, or any other wild thing, to go on having to depend on humans, would you?'

'No,' I agreed. 'And we couldn't go on feeding it for ever, because we'll be going away again some day.'

We had reached the dry stone wall which bounded the trees near the edge of the little tarn.

'Look!' exclaimed Jan, pulling up short, and pointing ahead.

There on the path stood the heron, erect and graceful and strong. As we watched it, it flexed its long, red legs, spread its huge wings, and rose slowly and powerfully into the air. It circled once over our heads; then, with the slowest and most ponderous wingbeats that I've ever seen, it skimmed over the frozen

'*Good-bye, Old Nod!*'

tarn, soared above the tree-tops beyond, and was lost to view.

'Good-bye, Old Nod!' I called, as it disappeared. 'Come back again, some day.'

'Well,' said Jan after a time (rather flatly, I thought). 'That's that!'

'Yes. Pity it should go when we'd collected such a spread for it. Shall we leave the scraps, d'you think?

The tarn's still frozen, so it can't catch anything there.'

'I expect it'll fish the becks for the present, where there's running water that doesn't freeze. Still, we might as well leave the things. He might come back, and I'd hate to disappoint him.'

So we spread the crusts and the fish skins – and even the fish meal – on the ground near the tree, as a nice surprise in case he returned.

'Look, Hyacinth,' said Jan, as we climbed back through the fir copse. 'I don't think we'll tell the others about this.'

'Right-ho,' I agreed. 'They might be rather cross that we'd not let them in on it sooner. Though I'm awfully surprised they weren't suspicious when you slipped away so jolly regularly.'

'Can't *all* be human bloodhounds like you!' chuckled Jan.

'Maybe not; but personally I found it remarkably fishy.'

'Fishy's the word! I've still got bits of sardine in my pockets.'

'I think, though, that you ought to write it down,' I said, 'for the holiday journal. It'd make an interesting chapter.'

'Mm,' said Jan, without any obvious enthusiasm.

'I'll do it if you like,' I offered. 'As a sort of thank-offering for being let in on it.'

'Would you really? That'd be fine, then. I've told you the whole story, so you'd be able to put everything in.'

'Right!' I said. 'I'll give the Blood-stained Hippo

a miss tonight, and get it all down while it's fresh in my memory.'

And that is what I've now done. No one else suspects anything. Won't they be surprised when they do eventually read it?

CHAPTER 8

Christmas Day in the Morning

WE had been having such a spell of brilliant weather when, in spite of the cold, we'd been able to spend so much of our time out of doors, that it didn't seem really like a December holiday, and Christmas came upon us unawares. Of course we had done most of our preparations during the term, so it didn't really matter when Christmas Eve arrived almost before we were expecting it.

It was a very active Christmas Eve. We wanted Mr and Mrs Jenks to be as free as possible for the celebrations so we did all that we could to help. Pat and Jan and I gave a hand outside, while Sally and Kay helped in the kitchen which, as you can guess was the centre of much activity. I don't believe that ever before have I seen a turkey, two ducks, and a chicken being cooked all at the same time; and Sally must have stirred many pounds of cake, and scone, and biscuit mixture. It was a job she liked, as it needed to be sampled frequently; and she and Mr Tiggle made a clean sweep of all the mixing bowls.

Pat and Jan and I finished by doing a quick dash over to the woods round Tarn Hows to gather holly before darkness came; and it proved to be quite a fruitful expedition, because Jan suddenly spied a snipe, boring for worms in the mud at the head of the tarn. We watched it for at least five minutes.

After tea we lounged on chairs, or lay on the hearth-rug, round the fire; and Mr and Mrs Jenks were there, too, which was fun. We roasted chestnuts,

Made a clean sweep of the mixing bowls

discovered strangers on the bars, and (after Sally had gone to bed) Mr Jenks told us a ghost story in broad Westmorland dialect. It was a jolly good story, too, but he told it so funnily that we all howled with laughter, and forgot to be frightened.

At eight o'clock Mrs Jenks suggested biscuits and bed for the rest of us.

'Don't suppose I'll go to sleep for *hours* yet,' I said. 'But it will make Christmas seem all the nearer if we go now, won't it?'

As a matter of fact I was quite wrong. Kay says that I never even answered when she called across her good night. So I must have gone to sleep the moment my head touched the pillow.

Pat and Kay slipped downstairs early the next morning, before the rest of us were awake; but Mr Jenks, bound on the same scheme, was even earlier.

When breakfast-time came the table was such a mass of parcels that it looked as though it would have to be a foodless meal. For once even Jan didn't seem to mind.

But Mrs Jenks did, and made an announcement.

'It's eat first, and unpack second,' she said firmly. 'Now put those parcels by until breakfast is over. You'll have all the rest of the day to look at them.'

So Pat and Jan and Kay stacked them in piles – Sally's on the window-seat, Kay's and mine on the dresser, Pat's on the rocking-chair, and Jan's on the cupboard – while Sally and I carried in the porridge.

We summoned up the most tremendous self-restraint, and didn't return to the parcels till we'd cleared away and washed up the breakfast things. Then we let ourselves go.

Most important of all were the ones from Mother and Father in India. We seemed to know by instinct which these were, and unpacked them at once.

'*Handbook of British Birds*, Volume Three,' announced Jan with satisfaction, getting at his first, and holding it aloft.

We could have guessed that in advance, of course. He is collecting the set, and Mother and Father send him one each Christmas.

'What's anyone else got?'

'A compass!' exclaimed Pat, opening a well-packed box, and discovering a most beautiful little instrument in a gun-metal case.

'That's fine, 'cos your other's a bit out of adjustment, isn't it?'

'Mm, and this is a beauty; it'll be awfully useful

when I sail the Atlantic single-handed. What's yours, Hyacinth?'

'I don't know, quite,' I said, pulling my present from its sheets and sheets of tissue paper. 'It's something silky, but I can't discover which is the beginning.'

'Why, it's a sari!' Kay exclaimed. 'A native Indian dress. Isn't it lovely – so soft, and such gorgeous shades of green and blue! Do hold it up in front of you. It's *just* the colour of your eyes.'

'See what I've got! Aren't they funny; two of them!'

'What are they, Sally? Oh, little wooden dolls, how nice. I expect they're hand-carved. And they're in native costume, too.'

'I should think one's a water-carrier, and one a dancing girl,' suggested Pat.

'I shall call them Kim and Moura,' declared Sally. 'What've you got, Kay?'

'A leather writing-case, exactly what I've been wanting for ages. I do think Mother and Father are clever to guess so well for all of us.'

Mr Jenks came in at that moment.

'How *did* these come?' demanded Jan. 'I swear the post van hasn't brought them since we've been here.'

'They came,' said Mr Jenks with the most solemn of expressions, 'one night, on a white elephant with ears as big as rhubarb leaves and tusks weighing eighty pounds apiece.'

'Ooh,' said Sally. 'I *do* wish I'd seen him.'

'He didn't arrive till after you were all in bed, and he was too big for the stable, so I had to put him in

A white elephant with ears as big as rhubarb leaves

the barn for the night. He left next morning very early, long before you were up. He'd got to go on to Spain as quickly as he could to pick up a cargo of peppercorn and pomegranates.'

'Did he leave anything for you?' Kay asked.

'Indeed he did,' said Mrs Jenks, coming in at that moment. 'He brought me this; it's just exactly what I wanted.'

She pointed to the brooch pinned into her dress, a pretty little one of enamel and silver.

The presents from India were the most exciting, but there were lots of others, too, useful thick walking-socks for all of us from Aunt G, maps, note-paper, pencils, books, and – best of all the lesser ones – book tokens. We don't waste time, when in Westmorland, thinking about London; but these, at least, did promise some pleasure for when we went back there.

By the time we'd finished unpacking there were mountains of brown paper and cardboard boxes, and a terrific litter of envelopes, tissue, and string.

'Next job,' said Pat firmly, 'is to get this room ship-shape. Hi, Jan! What are you doing stuffing all those papers into the cupboard? Fold them up properly and put them into piles, brown paper into this box and tissue into the other. Try to untie all knots in the string.'

Pat, of course, is a stickler for having things packed neatly, and into the smallest possible space. I suppose it is in readiness for when he goes to sea, and has to keep everything he possesses in a hammock and sea-chest – or whatever it is they're allowed.

'I can't fold mine,' said Sally. ''Cos Mr Tiggle's sitting on them.'

'Then you must shoo him off. Hi, Mr Tiggle, move along there, please!'

Mr Tiggle looked coldly at Pat, got up slowly, and moved away with tremendous dignity. The last we saw of him was a very erect tail rounding the sitting-room door.

'Oh, *poor* Mr Tiggle!' said Sally. 'You *have* hurt his feelings, Pat. He'll be awfully starchy for the rest of the day.'

'Can't be helped,' said Pat cheerfully. 'I bet he's forgotten by dinner-time. If not, I'll share my turkey leg with him. Now, about this clearing –'

'Let's stack our presents in separate piles,' suggested Kay. 'Look, Sally, yours'll fit nicely on the window-seat.'

We made a really good job of the tidying. Then it was time to put on our outdoor things, and, with Mr

Jenks, to walk the two and a half miles to Brathay Church for the Christmas morning service. We went by Skelwith Bridge, and came back, mostly uphill, through Skelwith Fold, Bull Close, and on to the Coniston road. That gave us a good five-mile round, and a huge hunger – which was just as well.

Mr Jenks carved the turkey magnificently, and seemed to find legs and wings, as well as all the extras, for everyone. Pat nobly remembered his promise to share, and Mr Tiggle forgot all about hurt dignity, and graciously accepted everything that was offered. The plum pudding, sprigged with holly, came in in procession, Mrs Jenks holding the dish aloft, and Sally following behind with the sauce-bowl. And how it was worked I can't imagine, but there was a shining new sixpence in every helping.

'What's everyone doing this afternoon?' asked Jan after we'd cleared away.

'What I *feel* most like doing,' I gasped, 'is lying flat on my back on the hearth-rug, and sleeping off a little of what I've eaten.'

'You'd be snoring like a stuffed pig, in five minutes,' said Pat. 'Much better *walk* it off.'

'Oh, let's!' exclaimed Kay. 'We'll feel a heap more lively when we've covered five miles or so.'

'Hadn't we better take Mr Tiggle, then?' said Jan. 'He's eaten so much that he'll never need to catch another mouse.'

'Don't you worry,' chuckled Mr Jenks. 'He'll be on the warpath this very night, if I know him right.'

Mr Tiggle settled the question for himself by curling up on the hearth-rug in front of the fire, and going firmly to sleep.

We dashed for our walking-shoes, and were away in five minutes. That walk was taken definitely for exercise, and Pat set a rattling pace, even though Sally was with us. We went down through the meadows and across the Oxenfell road, climbed steeply to Hodge Close, followed the path through the juniper scrub, dropped down to Tilberthwaite quarries, cut over on to the Tilberthwaite road, turned left to the mouth of Yewdale, and came back by the steep scramble up Glen Mary to Tarn Hows and home through the woods.

We reached the fell farm at four, more nearly hungry than we'd thought we would ever be again.

CHAPTER 9

Here We Come A-wassailing

CHRISTMAS tea was a leisurely meal, eaten inform-
ally round the fire, while Farmer Jenks told stories of
other winters at High Tarn, of deep snow and hard
frost, of parties and carols and waits.

'Let's go down to Farmer Wetherby's and sing
carols outside his door!' suggested Jan.

'Ooh, may we? It's a beautifully starry night, and
it'd feel *so* Christmassy.'

'May I go, too?' begged Sally.

'*Please* do let her,' said Kay, as Mrs Jenks looked
doubtful. 'We'll promise not to stay long, and we'll
get back before her bedtime.'

'Why don't we all go?' suggested Farmer Jenks
suddenly. 'Leave the dogs in charge up here. There's
nothing more to be done tonight.'

'We-ll, I don't know. It's years since I went carol
singing –'

'Oh, *do* come,' we begged. 'It'd be lovely. And we'd
sing *so* much better with you and Mr Jenks to help us.'

'All right, then; I'll get the guard for this fire. Put
on your top-coats and scarves, all of you. It's freezing
keen again tonight.'

In five minutes we were ready to set out. Mr Jenks,
who had gone across to the barn, came back with a
storm lantern which he lighted. It wasn't really necessary, because we could every one of us have found
our way in pitch darkness and blindfolded; but he
said that it made us look like real waits.

We sang the carols over to ourselves, very softly, as

we tramped down to Skelwith Bridge, just to make sure that we remembered words. At Plover Rigg we placed the lantern on the ground inside the porch, and made a semicircle round it.

'Good gracious, Sally!' exclaimed Kay, catching sight of the infant in the lamplight. 'Whatever's that you've got in your scarf?'

'It's Mr Tiggle,' explained Sally. 'He seemed to want to come, too; and I didn't think he ought to have his feelings hurt twice in one day.'

'Well, I'm blowed –!' said Pat.

'Maybe he'll help with the carols,' chuckled Farmer Jenks. 'Put him down in the front row, Sally. Now are you all ready? Then –'

So, with Mr Jenks to count us in, we started on 'The First Nowell'.

Half-way through the verse the door opened, and in the brightness inside were Farmer and Mrs Wetherby and Bill.

'Waits, indeed!' said Farmer Wetherby as we finished the last verse. 'Now that makes it really Christmas. Step over, all of you, won't you?'

'And take off your coats and scarves and mitts,' said Mrs Wetherby as Mr Tiggle led us over the threshold, 'so that you'll feel the good of them when you go; and draw up to the fire.'

She disappeared towards the kitchen, while Farmer Wetherby threw fresh logs on to a fire that was already crackling brightly, and Bill helped to find chairs and stools for all of us.

Just as soon as we were settled Mrs Wetherby was back with tray, tall bottle, glasses, and a Christmas cake that was practically still all there.

'It's my own, home-made elderberry wine,' she said. 'And it'll do you no harm at all after that cold walk you've had.'

In fact I think it must have done us good. I know that I felt a lovely, warm glow spreading through me after I'd finished mine.

Started on 'The First Nowell'

'Please, could Mr Tiggle have a drop, too?' begged Sally. 'Case *he* felt the cold coming down.'

'Careful, now,' advised Farmer Jenks with a twinkle. 'We don't want him to miss the mice, you know.'

'He'd be seeing them twice over and wouldn't know which one to go after,' suggested Bill.

'I fancy Mr Tiggle would rather have milk,' said

Mrs Wetherby. 'Fetch him a drop from the dairy, will you, Bill? Get that brown saucer that Sooty used to have.'

'Aye, and bring your fiddle downstairs, too, Bill. A tune will help if we're going to sing carols.'

So when he had put down the brown saucer brimming with milk, and Mr Tiggle, purring with satisfaction, had walked all round it twice, and then settled down to it in earnest, Bill went upstairs for his fiddle. He tuned up while we finished our cake and lingered over the wine.

'*Lovely*,' I sighed, nearly standing on my head to drain the very last drops from my glass. 'What are we going to sing?'

'"Good King Wenceslas" first.'

So we sang that, and then 'Silent Night', and afterwards 'We Three Kings'.

'Couldn't we have one from Sally?' asked Farmer Wetherby.

'I don't think she knows one well enough, do you, Sally?' said Kay doubtfully.

'Yes I do. I know "Away in a manger". And I think I'd sing it better without any music.'

'Right you are: I'll pipe down,' agreed Bill.

'Away in a manger, no crib for a bed,
  The little Lord Jesus laid down His sweet head.
  The stars in the bright sky looked down where He lay,
  The little Lord Jesus asleep on the hay.

'The cattle are lowing, the Baby awakes,
  But little Lord Jesus no crying He makes.
  I love Thee, Lord Jesus! Look down from the sky,
  And stay by my side until morning is nigh'

sang Sally, really quite surprisingly nicely, in a little, high voice.

'Very good indeed, Sally,' said Mrs Wetherby. 'Now, what's the next one?'

'The "Cuckoo Carol", please,' I suggested. 'But not just me alone.'

After that Jan asked for 'Ding Dong Merrily on High', and Pat chose 'Past Three O'clock'.

'And that'll have to be the very last one, I think,' said Mrs Jenks. 'It's Sally's bedtime in half an hour. Just time to get back.'

It would have been lovely to have stayed really late; but bedtime – especially Sally's – is one of the things Mrs Jenks is firm about. We tugged on our outdoor things and relit the storm lantern. The Wetherbys stood at the door, with the lamplight behind them.

'Good-bye!' we called, as we went out into the frosty, starlit night. 'Thank you for that lovely wine and cake and everything.'

'Welcome, welcome!' boomed Farmer Wetherby, while Mrs Wetherby added, 'And see that you're here for it again next Christmas.'

'That would be *grand!* Good-bye!'

'Good-bye, good-bye!' we could still hear Bill's voice after we were through the gate.

I was surprised to find how sleepy I was when we got back to High Tarn. Perhaps it was the walk uphill under the stars that did it. Sally was bustled upstairs at once, and soon afterwards Jan and I were packed off, too.

'Off you go, both of you,' said Mrs Jenks. 'Jan's yawned ten times in two minutes, and Hyacinth can scarcely keep her eyes open.'

D

'Can't think why,' I said, making a tremendous effort to collect my wandering thoughts, ''cos I don't really want Christmas to come to an end.'

'It's that elderberry wine!' chuckled Mr Jenks. 'And I think Sally must have given Mr Tiggle a drop of hers, after all. Look at him curled up on that cushion! The mice'll have it all their own way tonight I guess!'

CHAPTER 10

A Walk of Some Importance

WE had spent the morning doing odd jobs about the farm for Mr Jenks. Kay had helped with the milking, and attended to the calves. Pat had carried a ton of hay – or so he said – from the farm to the meadows below. Sally had gathered up the eggs and put down

Bagged our usual job

saucers of milk (for the barn cats, really, but I saw Mr Tiggle having the first lap at each one).

Jan and I had bagged our usual job, which Mr Jenks calls 'Mucking out the chickens'. Kay says that she can't imagine why we should find cleaning out all the hen huts in the little intak so vastly amusing, and Pat swears that our roars of laughter nearly shake the plates off the dresser in the kitchen. But Mr Jenks

thinks that we make a jolly good job of it, and says
he doesn't mind how soon we want to do it again.

So, in one way and another, we all got up rattling
good appetites, ate a hearty dinner, and then found
ourselves at a loose end, and with masses of energy to
spare.

'I vote we walk,' suggested Kay, as we got on with
the washing-up.

'Ooh, let's!' I said. 'It's a most wonderful day;
we'll be able to see everything for miles around.'

'Too late to get any great distance, though; it'll
be dark in about three hours.'

'Oh yes,' agreed Kay. 'I didn't mean a real expedition, just a walk – on roads more or less. We can
do an eight- or nine-mile round easily before tea-
time.'

'I'm game,' said Pat. 'Where d'you vote we go?'

'What about Elterwater first?' suggested Jan. 'We
haven't been over in that direction much this time.'

'Right-ho! Then Skelwith Bridge by the field path
and along the river.'

'Up to Spy Hill and over the rough land to the
Barngate road.'

'On to Borwick Lodge, and home by Tarn Hows.'

'Fine!' exclaimed Jan. 'Let's finish off these things
as quickly as we can. *Do* buck up with those plates,
Hyacinth; you're being awfully fussy about streaks
today.'

'You'll finish them off once and for all if you try to
be too speedy,' declared Pat. 'And by the way, what
about Sally? Bit too concentrated for her, isn't it?'

'That's all right,' said Kay. 'Mrs Jenks is having a
baking afternoon, and the infant wouldn't miss it for

anything. 'Fact she's up to the eyes, more or less, in the flour bin already.'

We finished the washing-up at a speed which satis-fied even Jan, and dashed off to get into sweaters and wind-jackets, thick socks and walking-shoes. There was obviously no need for rain-coats. In fact it was such a brilliant day that we felt it might never rain again – quite a cheering thought in the Lake District, though we were hoping for a good, hefty snowfall sometime during the holiday.

We clattered into the kitchen to say good-bye (and to sample the first batch of biscuits, just coming out of the oven), then dashed away down the steep path through the pine trees and the rocky meadow to the high road.

This helter-skelter progress is a very bad thing, really. Keeping up a steady pace, rather on the slow side, is the fell-man's most important rule. But it is an understood thing with us that we gallop down this first bit (not more than half a mile at the most), just as we like. It uses up our first wild energy, so that by the time we reach the road we are ready to settle down to our steady pace.

It happened like that today, and in five minutes' time we were swinging along the Oxenfell road in good formation and chatting quite calmly.

First we took a roll-call of all the peaks in view. We do that two or three times every holiday, from various points, just to refresh our memories, and to be certain that we don't forget any of the less obvious ones.

'The Old Man and Wetherlam back left,' said Pat. 'Then Crinkles, Pike O' Blisco and Bowfell.'

'Pike O'Stickle, Harrison Stickle, High White Stones, Silver How and Loughrigg Fell.'

'A tiny scrap of Skiddaw – or is that Blencathra? Then Helvellyn, Dollywagon Pike and Fairfield.'

'Red Screes, High Street, Ill Bell, Harter Fell, and Wansfell in front of them.'

We swung left on to the Colwith road, so steep at this point that it was hard not to break into a wild gallop.

'The river's jolly low,' I remarked, as we crossed the bridge.

'They've had an awfully dry autumn, Farmer Jenks says.'

'Wait till there's been some snow. I guess it'll swirl down here when the thaw comes!' said Jan with relish. He was probably imagining bridges capsizing, and sheep and cattle being swept away. He never believes in doing things by halves – even when they are disastrous ones. We didn't bother to remind him that most of these bridges are old pack ones, and have stood up to storm and flood and such things for hundreds of years.

Two miles farther, just on the fringe of Elterwater village, we turned in at the gate to the field path along the river and through the woods and meadows to Skelwith Bridge.

The ground was dry and frosty underfoot, and the pine needles and the fallen cones gave a nice, resiny smell as we brushed through them. There was a tang of wood smoke, too, and a thin, almost transparent column went straight up into the air from somewhere over a knoll where they were burning brush-wood. The tarn was almost completely iced over, but, at the far side, we could see a patch of open water, brilliantly blue, and with at least a dozen great white swans on it. Elterwater is, of course, one of their wintering haunts.

'I don't believe they're mutes,' said Jan. 'I saw them alighting the other day, and I'm sure I heard them hooting.'

'Whoopers, d'you suppose?'

'Probably, though they *might* be Bewicks.'

Jan is given to making wildly hopeful statements about many things; but on the subject of birds he is really jolly sound, so we were quite prepared to believe him.

'Pity it's so difficult to get right to the edge of Elterwater,' said Kay, 'especially on the far side.'

'Mm! I've been scouting about to try to find a spot near enough to watch them.'

'Take care that you don't get frozen in like the heron,' I said; and grinned inwardly at Pat's and Kay's puzzled expressions.

At Skelwith Bridge we came out on to the main road, but forked left almost at once to Spy Hill and Skelwith Fold. The rough land – across from Skelwith Fold to near Bull Close on the Barngate road – is a specially good place for holly. We saw several trees simply covered.

'They're lovely this year, aren't they?' said Kay. 'Mr Jenks would probably predict a hard winter.'

By the time we reached the Barngate road the full brilliance of the day was over, and there was the first hint of dusk.

'This road always gives me the shivers a bit,' I said, 'even in midsummer, and at midday.'

'I know,' agreed Kay. 'It seems miles from any-where, and those trees are so jolly gloomy, specially with the fell going up steeply and rockily just behind.'

'Fact,' said Jan, 'anything might happen here!'

'Something *has* happened! Whatever's that lorry doing drawn right in there, hidden in the trees?' I exclaimed, standing stock-still in surprise.

'*Come on!*' *Pat hissed*

'Come on!' Pat hissed, suddenly. 'Don't stand there staring; and don't ask any questions. Just go on talking normally, all of you, as though nothing had happened.'

Kay rose to the occasion valiantly with the most ordinary of remarks as we walked steadily on.

'I do think the view over this heathy land and on to Windermere, with the High Street mass behind, is one of the most satisfactory I know,' she announced.

'Yes,' Pat agreed, 'especially with all those birches scattered about.'

'And one of the really good places for hearing curlews,' said Jan.

We had gone at a good pace, covered quite a distance from the spot where we'd seen the lorry, and rounded a bend.

'Well!' Pat exclaimed.

'But what's it all about, Pat? Is there something wrong?' I demanded.

'I'm ready to swear there is, though I can't tell you what.'

'But why –?'

'Well, did you see that fellow near the lorry? No, I thought not – he sort of melted into the trees when he noticed us. And I think there was another one, too. I'm certain there's something fishy going on, though I can't for the life of me think what it can be.'

'What ought we to do about it then?'

'I don't know. But it certainly wouldn't have done any good to hang about and look as though we were spying on them, or poking into their affairs.'

'No, of course not. But I do wish we could think what they were there for. There didn't seem any point in having a lorry in among those trees, did there?'

'It was a cattle truck, actually, wasn't it?' said Jan. 'Perhaps it's a stolen one, and they're trying to hide it till all the flap's over.'

'Maybe,' Pat agreed. 'Well, we know where it is, and I don't think they realized that we'd seen them.'

'No,' I said. 'You certainly ordered us on pretty slickly!'

We talked about it most of the way to Borwick, and along the mountain road home, but without really reaching any solution. It was just settling down to darkness as we swung up through the firs by the short track from the mountain road to High Tarn.

Naturally there was a tremendous tea waiting. We gave it our full attention, and quite forgot about the lorry incident. It was not until later in the evening that the problem was solved with a bang.

CHAPTER II

Back After Nightfall

SALLY had gone to bed, and the rest of us were basking in front of a glowing log fire, with the lovely, relaxed feeling of exertion well and truly over (and a good tea well and truly eaten), when we heard Farmer Jenks talking to Mrs Jenks in the kitchen.

We weren't eavesdropping, because there was nothing private in the conversation; in fact he was speaking very loudly as he does on the few occasions when he's really wrathful. He had just come back from Farmer Wetherby's place, and was full of something he had heard there.

'Well, they're at it again,' we heard him say angrily.

'Who are, and at what?' asked Mrs Jenks.

'Sheep rustlers,' boomed Mr Jenks. 'Will Longmire says there are at least a score of his gone from the rigg, and some of Wetherby's are missing, too.'

'But however do they manage to get away with them?'

'Wish I could tell you that; they certainly know how to handle sheep – and in the darkness, too! Must have a dog to do the rounding up, I suppose, and some sort of truck to carry them off. No one seems to be able to find any traces of them, though; and they never work the same fells two nights together.'

I suppose it was the mention of the truck that rang a bell in Pat's memory. He sat up with a jerk.

'Well, I'm blowed!' he exclaimed in astonishment. 'So *that*'s who they were!'

'Which who, and were what?' asked Kay, lazily prodding an ash log till it sent up a shower of sparks.

'The fellows we saw this afternoon, skulking in the woods with the cattle truck.'

It was funny what a difference that made. In half a jiffy we were sitting upright in a close circle round the fire, very much alert. Kay and Jan had tumbled to it immediately; but I still felt rather vague.

'But what *are* rustlers? And what do they rustle?'

'Sheep-stealers,' Pat explained. 'They come and nab them in the night, and when they've got them away they change the markings so that they can't be identified.'

'Gracious!' I exclaimed. 'And we walked right past them this afternoon. If only we'd realized –'

Pat shook his head. 'We couldn't have done anything then, even if we'd known, could we?'

'No, I suppose not.'

'But do you realize where they were? In the woods just on the edge of Black Fell. If they're on the job tonight it'll be Farmer Jenks' sheep they're stealing.'

'Whew!' whistled Jan. 'What'd we better do? Oughtn't we to tell him?'

'We-ll, I don't know,' said Pat. 'Couldn't we tackle this ourselves? After all, we're not dead sure we're right, and I'd hate to raise a false alarm.'

'But if we *are* right?'

'Well, there are four of us, and we have the advantage over the rustlers, because we know all about them and where they are, but they have no idea that we know.'

'It'll mean doing something this very night.'

'Yes, of course. That's partly why I think we ought to tackle it alone. It'd waste so much valuable time if we had to go into long explanations. How's the moon; does anyone know?'

'Fairly new. Sets about midnight, I believe,' said Kay.

'Mm! That gives us a few hours. They won't start work seriously till it's nearly gone, I shouldn't think.'

We weren't lounging and relaxed any longer, not one of us. We sat in a tight circle round the fire, and held a council of war. In less than half an hour our plans were complete.

Sally had been in bed for some time, and, by now, was probably sleeping soundly. When Mrs Jenks came bustling in some time later she found us all yawning widely, as though bogged with sleepiness.

'It's all that fresh air and walking,' she said. 'You're none of you more than half awake. You'd better have your milk and biscuits now, and get to bed early for a long night's rest.'

'Oh, *please* could we?' I said, yawning tremendously. 'I don't think I could possibly keep my eyes open for more than another ten minutes.'

I saw the shade of a grin flicker across Jan's face at the thought of a long night's rest; but it was gone again in a moment. We all managed to keep up the sham pretty well, and in next to no time we were drinking the hot milk that Kay had boiled, and munching the nice, thick digestive biscuits which Mrs Jenks thinks are not too rich to go to bed on.

I believe we were through that supper in record time (it is a meal we generally spin out to the limit). Then we said our good nights, mingled with a few suitable yawns, and trooped off upstairs – but not to sleep, nor even to bed.

In fact we were determined that within the hour we would be away on the mountain road past Tarn Hows, haring along in the frosty moonlight. The thought gave me a shiver down my spine – not only because of the chillness of the night.

Yawning tremendously

Up in our room Kay and I quietly rooted out our togs, our warmest sweaters, wind-jackets, mitts, thick socks, and gym shoes. Then we crept quietly across the landing, and slipped silently through the door of the boys' room. They were nearly ready.

'What about balaclava helmets?' suggested Jan. 'It's *frigid* outside.'

'Not on your life!' said Pat firmly. 'You'll have to keep your ears absolutely skinned on tonight's job. Ready, everyone?'

There is never any difficulty about getting out unseen, for Pat and Jan share the small room at the back, the only one with a window on that side, and the rocky knoll comes up to within a foot of the sill. So it is almost as easy as going through the front door – though, of course, much more fun.

Pat went first, and I followed. Jan came third (leaving a neat segment of his trouser seat on the window-catch), and Kay was last. I don't know why, but that is generally our single file order.

At first we crept along with tremendous care. It was so dark, and so very quiet, that a cracking stick sounded like a pistol shot, and a tumbling stone like a thunderbolt. But once we were clear of the farm we quickened speed.

Actually our shortest way would have been directly up the hill from High Tarn, across the top of Black Fell, and down straight into the woods on the far side. But there was no real track, and though we were pretty sure that we could have found our way, even in the dark, the drop at the other side would have been terribly difficult. It is largely steep, rough scree, with trees and scrubby undergrowth, and we should have been jolly lucky to get down without making a tremendous clatter and giving the whole show away.

So we decided to do the long way round – down the cart track from the farm to the Tarn Hows road, sharp left and along the two miles of that to where it joins the Barngate one, then straight ahead to the spot where we'd seen the cattle truck, somewhere between the Barngate Inn and Bull Close.

It was a stretch of at least four or five miles, but it

meant that we should approach along a road, absolutely silently as we were wearing rubbers, and of course we'd be able to hare along for much of the way.

We saved most of our wind for the running, and didn't waste any on conversation, which wasn't necessary, anyhow, for we'd made all plans in that thirty-minute council of war round the fire.

Saved our wind for the running

'D'you remember your jack-knife, Jan?' Kay asked, as we slipped through the gate on to the Tarns road.

'Rather: it's jolly sharp, too; I did it on the whetstone yesterday.'

'I say, which way *does* a screw turn?' I panted, as we jogged down a steep bend.

'Clockwise to screw, anticlock to unscrew, usually.'

We turned left at the foot of the slope, and sped on

in a tight bunch in the darkness. A mile or so on, somewhere beyond the inn, Pat gave the warning.

'Nearly up to the wood. We'd better walk the rest. and not speak another word. You all remember the signals and arrangements, don't you?'

'Mm!'

'Yes, rather!'

'All O.K.? Then come on.'

We crept along in single file but almost touching each other, and slipped into the trees not far from the remote spot where we'd seen the cattle truck.

The moon had gone, though it wasn't quite so late as Kay had said, and it was as dark as – well, as dark as night, and jolly eerie. An owl hooted suddenly, and I'm very much afraid that I gave a startled little gasp. But I think that was just about the only sound we made as we crept forward, inch by inch, through the trees.

CHAPTER 12

Rustlers

SUDDENLY, and sooner than I'd expected, Pat froze, crouching low in the undergrowth. I guessed that we must be pretty close to the truck, and I screwed my eyes for all I was worth, trying to focus them in the darkness.

And, by degrees, I began to make things out – very dimly, and partly by guess-work – the massive shape of the cattle truck, perhaps not more than twenty feet away, and two (possibly three) figures stealthily moving about. Then I realized there were other dim forms, too, a whole bunch of them, low on the ground; and one of them suddenly gave a soft, trembling bleat. They were the sheep that had been rounded up, and I guessed that every single one of them would have the ear clips, the H.T. branded on the fleece, and a great tar daub on the left shoulder, to show they belonged to High Tarn and Farmer Jenks.

It seemed to be getting a little lighter, though I suppose it was merely my eyes growing accustomed to the darkness of the wood. I could see now that they were in the middle of loading. I think there was a dog somewhere (though it never gave so much as a single yelp), for the sheep were in a tight bunch, and were being gradually edged towards the truck, a tricky business in the darkness.

One of them stepped on to the wooden gangway. There was a sharp scuffle as it was seized, and heaved bodily in; then, with a sudden stampede the rest were after it, and in a moment were all inside. The slam of the gate into position, and the sound of the bolt being shot home were the first really definite noises we'd heard.

It must have been a tremendous relief to the rustlers to have finished that part of the job, and I could hear them breathing heavily after the exertion. Then the dark figures moved stealthily to the front of the truck; I think the dog jumped into the cab first, and the men followed. There was a faint squeak of the hinges as the door was swung too, and then the click of the catch.

And that, for us, was zero hour.

Pat, from in front, gave the signal we had arranged, a very low whistle that might have been one of the night birds, and was followed by our three answering whistles, equally faint, from the rear. At once we were on the move, creeping silently forward through the undergrowth.

It took us at the most, I suppose, half a minute to reach the wagon; but it felt like a century, and I had a dreadful feeling that they would start off suddenly, leaving us standing – and looking very silly.

But actually nothing like that happened. I expect they were eating what they considered a well-earned snack; and probably, too, caution and quietness were to them at this point more important than speed. Anyhow they just stayed put and gave us our chance. I can assure you we took it!

I knew Pat was only just ahead of me, but it was so difficult to see anything that, in the end, I almost walked bang into him when he stopped at the back of the truck where he was to deal with the bolts and the hurdles. I veered left, feeling my way round with my finger-tips.

My job was to do what I could with the valves on the left-hand side wheels. I can't pretend that I know a great lot about mechanics, but I got hopefully to work on the first of them. It came unscrewed in no time. There was a faint hiss of escaping air, and the lorry gave quite a lurch as it settled down on to the flat tyre. That set my heart absolutely banging in fright, because I didn't see how the rustlers could possibly have missed feeling it, and I listened with an awful, sickening certainty that I'd spoilt the whole show. But no sound came from the cab. Perhaps they thought the lurching was just the sheep moving about inside; or maybe they were too interested at that moment in their tuck-tin.

When the pounding inside me had abated a bit, and I'd gathered up my scattered wits (I'd forgotten, in my fright, that Pat had said speed was the thing to aim at) I crept on to the next wheel.

My success with the first wheel had been beginner's luck. The second valve was a demon. I seemed to go on struggling for centuries, but I just couldn't budge it, and it was all becoming rather like a nightmare.

The darkness and the stillness made it seem so terribly lonely. I wondered how the others were getting on. There had been scarcely a sound from them, except for a very faint noise of slashing which I knew was Jan dealing with the tyres with his jack-knife, Once I thought that he crept by me, quite close, and I believed wriggled underneath, but I could only sense his passing, not really see him.

I was still struggling when I heard three very faint,

low whistles – the recall signal – and I knew that that second tyre had beaten me.

I groped my way round the truck to the back, and found the others already there. I guessed they'd all managed their parts perfectly.

'Can't unscrew the second,' I breathed as silently as I could when I joined them.

'Never mind, we've done enough. Jan's slashed all he could lay hands on,' whispered Pat, who was holding the back hurdle in position. 'Now then, I'll give you ten seconds to get clear before I let this down. O.K.?'

We slid into the darkness like shadows dissolving, making our separate ways to the point on the road where we'd arranged to link up. I think, now, that was the most eerie part of the whole adventure – the feeling of being so utterly alone, and yet knowing there were others moving not far away in the darkness. I counted seconds in my head as I crept away, so that I should have some idea of when the balloon was likely to go up.

'Hal-i-fax-one, Hal-i-fax-two –' It is a rough, but reasonably accurate, method we use, and I came to 'Hal-i-fax-ten' just at the moment when I crept out of the trees, and down the grassy bank on to the road.

I expected the most terrific hullabaloo then and there. But there was no sound, except, maybe, for a few, faint, muffled noises. I stood still, and wondered whether things had gone badly astray, and whether I ought to turn back. Then I remembered how Pat had said that, as we'd be working in complete darkness, the most important thing was for each one of us to stick absolutely to the plan. So I skimmed stealthily on down the road towards the far turning where we'd arranged to meet.

Kay and Jan were already there, though I didn't see them until I'd charged head on into Jan, and he'd let out the most awful startled yelp. But it didn't matter because, at that moment, the balloon *did* go up with the most glorious racket.

Pat told us afterwards that he'd had a fearful job to stir up the sheep. They seemed quite dazed by what had happened, and when, at the end of the ten seconds, he'd let down the drawbridge they hadn't made the least attempt to escape. In the end he'd crept up into the wagon, taken hold of the nearest ewe, and heaved and butted her down the slope into the dead bracken.

That started things all right. In a split second the rest of the sheep were charging down to freedom; and Pat was charging with them. You can guess that he didn't wait about to see what would happen next, but shook himself free from the woolly tidal wave, and came on at the double through the trees. This time he didn't have to think about being silent. The sheep were making an appalling uproar, splintering branches and crackling dead bracken as they scattered to freedom.

And the rustlers, too, had forgotten about caution. We heard the cab door flung open, the men jump out, and a burst of angry exclamations and oaths as they realized what was happening. As far as we could judge from those, our plans had been completely successful, and we were absolutely dancing with glee by the time Pat came haring along like a black shadow in the slightly less black night.

'Let's give them a war-cry to finish!' suggested Jan.

'O.K.!' Pat grinned. 'Are you ready? Then one – two – three – *GO!*'

It would have been awful enough in the daylight, but coming unexpectedly out of the night, and just after all the pandemonium we'd let loose round their truck, it must have sounded simply horrific to those rustlers. We hoped so, anyhow, but naturally we weren't waiting about to see. As the sound of our yells died away, we turned with one accord, and raced along the road in the direction of home; and we didn't slacken pace till we'd put something like a good mile between ourselves and that gloomy wood.

It is funny how sleepy you can find yourself when once excitement is over, even though you are lolloping along at a good, steady jog-trot. We all suddenly discovered that we'd the most tremendous longing for our beds, and those seemed *miles* away. We yawned quite often, and didn't speak much.

'Golly!' chuckled Jan, in one of his wakeful moments. 'I'd like to see their faces when they try to make a quick getaway. I slashed those tyres to ribbons!'

As we turned up the Tarn Hows road Kay gave a sudden exclamation.

'Gracious! I'd forgotten all about these!'

She pulled four large digestive biscuits – crumby, but otherwise unscathed – from her pocket. That was a blessed moment.

I can't remember much more about the homeward run. There was the Tarn Hows road, the turn at the farm gate, the last, uphill jog through the trees, and then we were scrambling through the little window again, this time from outside.

'G'night,' whispered Jan, as Kay and I slipped quietly through the door on the landing. '*Please* someone waken me in time for breakfast.'

We crept safely across the landing and into our own room.

'Mrs Jenks *will* be astonished when we're still sleepy after a good night's rest, won't she?' said Kay, chuckling and yawning at the same time.

I *may* have replied to her; I don't know. All I can remember after that is – *sleep*.

CHAPTER 13

Daylight Investigation

IN spite of the night's activities, we were all down at the usual time next morning – which shows what a good wakener-up a spongeful of icy water can be. But after a few hours' sleep, that midnight adventure seemed as unreal as a dream; and we couldn't re-assure ourselves by discussing it at breakfast, for Sally was there, and we all felt that Mr Jenks ought to be first to hear.

'I say,' I whispered, as the infant ran off to the kitchen for more milk. 'I suppose we *did* hare along that mountain road past Tarn Hows in the night? It *wasn't* a dream, was it?'

'Judging by Jan's yawns *something* certainly happened,' said Kay.

'Oh golly!' chuckled Jan stifling another outsize in yawns. 'Those tyres – and the way the sheep thrashed about – and the noise they made –!'

'I guess the rustlers are wishing it had only been a dream.'

'Ssh!' Pat hissed. 'Here's the infant back. Let's drop the subject till we've finished washing up.'

We got through breakfast quickly (it is always a business-like meal, not one we linger over) and likewise the clearing and washing-up. Then when we'd finished, and Sally had give Mr Tiggle his saucer of milk, and they'd both gone off with the scraps for the chickens, the four of us trooped off to the barn where we could hear Mr Jenks tinkering about with some of his machinery.

'Hullo there!' he said, bringing his head up from the innards of the tractor, and grinning broadly at us all standing round in a circle. 'This a deputation?'

'*This a deputation?*'

'Sort of,' I agreed.

'Er – about those rustlers –' Pat began.

'Oh ay.' Mr Jenks wrestled with a large spanner and an obstinate nut. 'I was telling Mrs Jenks about them last night. Pretty bad they were last year, and seems that they've been round and about again. Well, we can only hope they don't work over Black Fell.'

'We think they were there last night.'

'What –!' roared Mr Jenks, dropping spanner and nut and everything.

'It's all right, though,' Pat said hurriedly. 'Because if they were we scotched them.'

Mr Jenks took off his old felt hat and scratched his head. Then he put down the hat on a bale of straw, and absent-mindedly sat down on it. We didn't enlighten him. That hat is put to many uses and never seems to come to any harm.

'Now then,' he said at last, planting his hands squarely on his knees. 'What's this you're telling me?'

We all began to speak at once, with much confusion.

'Pat, you explain, right from the beginning,' suggested Kay.

So we three fell silent, while he told Mr Jenks the whole story, about our afternoon walk and the wagon we'd seen in the woods, about our scheme for the night and how we'd carried it through. We didn't interrupt once. He explained everything exactly right.

'Well!' said Mr Jenks, when Pat had finished. 'You certainly *do* seem to have scotched them last night. But why didn't you say something about it earlier? You might have come to harm, you know – they're pretty desperate characters, those rustlers; and besides, we could perhaps have got the police on to the job, and caught them.'

'We-ll,' said Pat, rather slowly. It was a question we'd been expecting, and a bit difficult to explain. 'Well, perhaps we ought to have told you; but, you see, we didn't realize what it was all about when we first saw the wagon. It was only when we heard you talking to Mrs Jenks about rustlers that it dawned on us.'

'And by that time it was long after dark,'

interrupted Kay. 'So even if we'd got the police they wouldn't have been able to see anything. And we weren't *really* sure that we'd guessed right.'

'Only we *thought* we had,' said Jan, 'and it would have been awful if they'd not believed us, or gone poking around with super torches and given the whole show away.'

'And we knew that if there *were* rustlers in that wood it'd be High Tarn sheep they were after – and we were jolly well determined they weren't going to get away with those.'

'So I really think we managed pretty well, don't you?' I said, with a smile that I hoped would win him over.

'Aye,' agreed Mr Jenks, perhaps a little reluctantly. 'You did very nicely. Well, I reckon the rustlers'll have made a getaway by now.'

'They won't have got their wagon away,' chuckled Jan. 'Not unless they've brought a crane and a break-down gang, and I don't think they'd want to do that.'

'No, that's so. We'd better step over and take a look at it. And then, I reckon, we'd better get hold of the police. Hyacinth, you run indoors and ask Mrs Jenks if you can have sandwiches for the five of us; it'll maybe be a longish job.'

'I'll come and help,' said Kay. 'We'll have them ready in no time.'

'Shouldn't tell them what it's all about; no use worrying them unduly. Just say we're going to look over the sheep on Black Fell, and ask if we can have dinner when we come in,' called Mr Jenks as we dashed off.

We were ready and away in under twenty minutes,

the sandwiches packed into two haversacks which Pat and Jan carried. This time, as it was broad daylight and didn't matter about noise, we were going by the shortest route, right over the top; so we'd changed into our nailed boots. Mr Jenks, carrying his shepherd's crook (a lovely one, over a hundred years old, and with a ram's-horn top), led the way up the fell-side from the farm-yard.

It was another grand day and, from the top, we could see for miles, right over Blelham Tarn and Claife Heights, and Esthwaite and Windermere. The colours were all so brilliant, and everything looked so clear and sparkling, it was hard to believe that, somewhere steeply below us, hidden among the fir trees, was the cattle wagon and the scene of our night's adventure. I think, at that moment, we all four of us began to have a horrible suspicion that the whole thing had been nothing but a dream – or a nightmare.

But the wagon was there all right, and I can tell you it looked pretty derelict. I think they must have had a shot at getting it away; but it hadn't been much use, and they'd only managed to wedge it further into a rut, and almost turn it over. The tyres, of course, were completely flat, and just about slashed to ribbons. I noticed Jan standing with hands deep in pockets, looking at his night's work as though he'd painted a masterpiece.

Mr Jenks pushed his hat well back, shook his head thoughtfully and scratched it slowly.

'You certainly made a job of it!' he said.

'We thought we'd better. We didn't want to give them the least chance of getting it away.'

'Mm! That wagon would have held forty sheep at least – if they had loaded up; though I don't suppose they'd have managed quite so many in the dark. Still, they could have got away with a tidy few.'

Mr Jenks seemed to be growing more and more approving of what we'd done.

'Er – I suppose we *do* have to tell the police?' Pat asked.

'Oh aye; we must do that. They'd find the wagon, sooner or later, and start making inquiries.' Mr Jenks' face creased into its usual cheery grin. 'Don't you worry about it. I'll see they understand how fine you all did last night!'

'O.K.!' Pat said, grinning too. 'What do we do about it? Telephone?'

'Mm! That's the best thing. It's a tidy stretch, though, back to High Tarn.'

'I know,' I said, suddenly remembering. 'There's a phone at Spy Hill, at Skelwith Fold; I've seen the wires. Shall I dash there? I'm sure they'd let us use it.'

'I'll come with you,' offered Pat. 'Anyone got any money?'

So Pat and I hared along the road and across the rough land, a mile or so, to Spy Hill, and rang up the police station at Ambleside. They seemed a bit slow on the uptake, but I expect it was really our fault for not explaining more carefully. It's such a long job, beginning from the beginning, when the other person knows nothing at all. Anyhow, they got the gist of it in the end, and said they'd send someone along straight away. We said 'Thank you' for the use of the phone, left the pennies with the small boy of the house, and raced back to rejoin the others.

There was nothing more we could do then, so we sat down in the sunshine at the edge of the wood, and ate sandwiches hungrily.

In about twenty minutes we heard the sound of a bell, and looked up to see a very large police constable just coming round the bend on a bicycle of normal size which seemed almost like a toy one

Sat and ate sandwiches

under his huge bulk. Rounding the bend, and heading downhill, and suddenly coming upon us, all at the same time, rather put him off his stroke, and he braked so hurriedly that he would certainly have shot over the handle-bars but for the fact that, being so large, he could put both outsize feet quite firmly on the ground while still sitting comfortably in the saddle.

I heard Jan suppress a giggle, and saw Kay kick his ankle sharply. The constable dismounted with dignity, probably to make up for his rather comical entry, and touched his cap to Mr Jenks.

'G'day,' he said. 'You'll be the party that's re-ported the abandoned cattle wagon?'

Mr Jenks said that we were, and asked whether he'd like us to lead him to it.

'Noa. There'll be a p'lice car along in a minit. My orders was to proceed to the nearest point on the road, an' wait,' said the constable. He leaned his bicycle against the hedge, and drew a note-book from somewhere inside his tunic. 'Noa need to waste time, though. I'll be takin' down names an' addresses, an' a few fac's while we're waitin'.'

It was tremendously interesting, and I listened eagerly and lapped it all up. It seemed such a good chance to glean a little 'local colour' for the Blood-stained Hippo; and I racked my brains to think how I could bring a very large constable, who licked his pencil between every second word, into the next chapter.

He hadn't got far, though, before a very shiny police car slid round the corner and drew to a stand-still. An officer got out, and after that things began to move a bit. We all trooped back to the lorry, and somehow – though I don't quite know how – Mr Jenks managed to separate himself and the officer from the rest of us. They talked together for a time, and I guessed that the story of our night's doings was being unfolded. We'd have given anything to know what was said. The officer looked across in our direc-tion, and grinned broadly once or twice. He seemed an awfully decent sort of man.

Anyhow, Mr Jenks must have done us proud, be-cause there were no awkward questions at all. He asked us to describe the rustlers, but that wasn't easy, because we'd only seen one very fleetingly in the afternoon, and the others simply as dark shadows in the night. We told him all we could.

They examined the lorry very carefully, though without touching the door or steering-wheel or anything.

'Maybe you'll track them down by the lorry,' Mr Jenks suggested.

'Possibly,' said the officer. 'But not very likely. I expect it's a stolen one, and with the number plates changed, too. Still it may give us a clue. We'll be able to discover where they stole it.'

'Aye. I reckon they're up to all sorts of tricks. Seems a pity if they get away, though,' said Farmer Jenks, looking around angrily at the tangles of wool on the broken branches, and the trampled bracken where his sheep had stampeded in terror during the night.

'Mm! It certainly does. Still, I don't think *you'll* be troubled again. I should say they'll keep away from these parts for a long time.' I saw him glance at the slashed tyres, and I'm sure there was just the ghost of a smile on his face.

We went back with him to the road. He gave the constable instructions about staying on duty until he'd sent down the experts – finger-print men, and breakdown gangs, I suppose. Then he climbed back into the car and was driven away. He saluted us all as it turned the corner, and we all waved frantically back.

Or, rather, Mr Jenks, Kay, Pat and Jan did the waving. I'm afraid that I was once again busy collecting local colour. I'd smiled at the constable, and mentioned handcuffs, and at once he had drawn a pair from his back pocket and shown me how to use them. Pat asked me afterwards whether it was the hippo itself I intended to manacle. I hadn't really got as far as planning that, but I must say I thought the constable was a very decent sort of man.

Once again collecting local colour

'Well,' said Mr Jenks, 'that's that, and it's time we were making tracks for home. It'll be dark in under two hours, and there's milking to do.'

We called our good-byes to the constable, and he grinned and called his in return. Then, when we'd climbed a little way up the fellside through the trees, we heard his huge voice bellowing after us that if the laal lassie would call at the p'lice station next time she was passing, he'd take her to look at the cells.

'Ooh, thank you!' I called. 'Would you *truly*? That'd be *terribly* useful!'

We scrambled on, and went over the top of Black Fell in the last brightness of the afternoon. There were sheep everywhere, the little, shaggy, grey-faced Herdwicks that, from the distance, look just like stones and boulders on the fellside. Mr Jenks leaned on his crook and looked at them with satisfaction.

'Must round them up tomorrow and see they've taken no harm,' he said. Then, after a moment, he added, 'And but for the four of you there'd have been fifty less of them hereabouts, today!'

Which made a very pleasant ending to the whole adventure.

CHAPTER 14

A Medal for Gallantry

'HAS anyone seen Mr Tiggle?' asked Sally one morning soon after breakfast.

We were still busy with chores, and no one took much notice.

'Has *anyone* seen Mr Tiggle?'

Jan whistled shrilly as he scraped mud from his boots in the porch. Pat was poring over a map, and Kay and I sorted the knives and forks and spoons into their separate compartments.

'I DO WISH YOU'D LISTEN TO ME!' roared Sally crossly.

'Can't help doing when you make *that* noise,' said Kay.

'Well then, *has* anyone seen Mr Tiggle!'

'Often,' said Jan.

'This morning?'

'No, I don't think so.'

'Well I'm sure he's lost,' said Sally. 'I put his milk down straight after breakfast, and he hasn't touched it. Mrs Jenks, please have you seen Mr Tiggle?'

'Mr Tiggle?' said Mrs Jenks, coming through from the larder. 'No, I don't believe I have.'

'Then he's missing,' moaned Sally. 'I'm *sure* he is.'

'He'll turn up, sooner or later, Sally,' comforted Mrs Jenks. 'He can look after himself well enough.'

'But he'll be frightfully hungry. Why, he usually laps up his milk soon's I've put it down – then goes and laps the barn cats' if I don't watch him. I'll go and see if I can find where he's got to.'

She ran off across the farm-yard towards the barn, and for the rest of the morning we met her at intervals, searching in the byre, and behind the pigsty, and in the little intak. She had to be called twice at dinner-time, and came in looking very worried and rather dirty.

'*Hasn't touched his milk*'

'Why, Sally,' said Mrs Jenks. 'Wherever have you been all morning?'

'Looking for Mr Tiggle,' said Sally unhappily. 'And I can't find him anywhere.'

'He'll be all right, young 'un,' said Mr Jenks comfortingly. 'Turn up before tea-time, I guess, looking mighty pleased with himself as usual.'

'So just run along and wash your hands, Sally,' said Mrs Jenks. 'And then come and eat your dinner before it gets cold.'

But Mr Tiggle *hadn't* turned up at tea-time, though

Sally spent the whole afternoon searching. Kay went to fetch her in at dusk.

'Mightn't he be in a trap?' she asked miserably.

'Not likely,' said Mr Jenks very firmly. 'There are no traps on *my* land.'

'He'll be *so* hungry,' gulped Sally, munching a very buttery crumpet. 'He's had nothing to eat all day.'

'He'll have caught a mouse, I dare say,' said Mrs Jenks. 'He can look after his own needs, can Mr Tiggle.'

Sally spent an unhappy and very restless evening, rushing off every time she thought of a new place to be searched – the store-room or the dresser cupboard, inside the grandfather clock or the trunks in our bed-room. But Mr Tiggle was still missing when she went to bed.

'You *will* come and tell me at once if he comes home – promise you will!' she begged.

'Right-ho,' said Pat. 'The minute he walks in.'

'Now don't worry, Sally,' said Mrs Jenks. 'He'll be quite all right – and back by morning, I'm sure.'

Sally went off miserably to bed, and the rest of us drew into a smaller semicircle round the fire.

'It *is* odd, though,' said Mrs Jenks, when the infant was safely upstairs. 'He wasn't about last night, either. In fact, I don't remember seeing him at all after tea yesterday.'

'You don't *really* think anything dreadful has happened to him, do you?' I asked anxiously. 'Sally'd never get over it if he'd come to any harm.'

'No, he'll be all right, I dare say; only it isn't like him, that's all. He's never gone off before.'

'A cat likes to walk by itself, sometimes,' said Mr Jenks (through the half of his mouth that wasn't biting his pipe). 'Mr Tiggle's felt the call of the wild, I expect. He'll come back when he begins to miss his saucer of milk and his warm spot on the boiler.'

The moon hadn't yet risen. Outside it was inky black, and icy; but indoors the fire crackled warmly. We settled down to our separate occupations, and for a long time there was silence.

'What's that?' Mrs Jenks spoke so suddenly that she made me jump.

'What's what?' we asked.

'That rattling noise. Sounded like the latch on the front door.'

''Twould be that, I expect,' said Mr Jenks. 'There's a nail come loose, I noticed. Meant to put it right to-day, but it slipped my memory. 'Twould rattle if a bit of a breeze caught it.'

'But there's no wind, tonight,' said Kay. 'It's as still as – as –'

'No, well I dare say one of the dogs banged it, then,' said Mr Jenks, comfortably. 'I'll put it right tomorrow.'

He threw another ash log on to the fire, so that a fountain of sparks shot up. We settled down again to our books and things – for ten minutes.

'There!' said Mrs Jenks, just as suddenly. But this time it didn't make anyone jump, for we had all heard the rattle. She put down her mending.

'I knew it was the front door, and that time it banged right to. Someone's left it open. I'll go and shut it.'

'I'll go,' said Pat, dropping his book and starting across the room.

But he never got very far, for suddenly the living-room door burst open, and there on the threshold stood Sally.

She was in her pyjamas – pink striped ones, bedroom slippers, and a bright, red jersey pulled on very

Mr Tiggle in her arms

hastily, back to front, I think. Her hair was tousled, her face and hands very dusty. She had a large tear in one pyjama leg – and Mr Tiggle in her arms.

'Sally!' we all exclaimed together, and then I added, 'And Mr Tiggle! Where *did* you find him?'

'In the loft,' gasped Sally, and burst into tears.

'Now then, young 'un,' said Mr Jenks, drawing Sally's favourite stool forward. 'That won't do! Come along and tell us all about it.'

Mrs Jenks was already leading her across to the fire.

'Let her get warm, first,' she said. 'It's no night to be out of doors in pyjamas – even if they *are* flannel ones. Kay, go and heat some milk on the stove, will you? And Pat, just run upstairs and fetch her dressing-gown – yes, and her sponge, too, and she can clean her hands and face a bit.'

'Warm some milk for Mr Tiggle, too, please,' gulped Sally. 'He's absolutely ravenous.'

'But *how* did you come to find him?' I asked.

'Well,' said Sally, 'soon after I'd gone to bed I remembered that yesterday afternoon we'd been in the stable when Mr Jenks was up in the loft with the trap-door open for *ever* such a long time. And I thought that Mr Tiggle might have gone up the ladder, and got fastened in when we came to tea.'

'There now! I knew I hadn't seen him since before tea yesterday,' said Mrs Jenks.

'Well, I went on thinking about it, and not going to sleep, and in the end I was *sure* he was there.'

'But why didn't you come to tell us?' asked Pat.

'We-ell,' said Sally, sipping the milk which Kay had brought, and already looking much warmer and rosier, 'I was afraid you'd all say wait till morning, and I was *certain* he was there, and he'd be so hungry.'

'He could always catch a mouse for himself,' suggested Jan. 'There are millions up there.'

'He'd be *thirsty*, anyhow,' said Sally indignantly. 'Just look how he's lapping up his milk. And he'd have no fresh air at all. So I decided I'd rescue him myself. I crept downstairs and out of the front door.'

'I *knew* I'd heard the latch!'

'I was afraid you would. I tried to be awfully quiet.'

'But however did you manage out there? It's pitch dark.'

'I – I borrowed Pat's torch. An' I think I may have broken the bulb, 'cos I dropped it on my way back, and it went out, and I couldn't find it.'

'We'll look for it tomorrow,' said Pat.

'And you went right up that ladder by yourself!' said Mrs Jenks. 'You oughtn't to have done that, you know, Sally. And however *did* you lift the trap-door?'

'It's a ton weight!' declared Mr Jenks.

'I thought I wasn't going to be able to – at first. But I pushed for all I was worth. I put the torch in my mouth, and I pushed with both hands and my head and one shoulder. And I just managed to lift it up a little way, and there was Mr Tiggle, and he squeezed through in a flash. I think he knew that I would come to rescue him, sooner or later.'

'Well, I think that's a very gallant act,' said Mr Jenks. 'Very gallant indeed. You deserve a medal for that, young 'un.'

'But you shouldn't have done it on your own, Sally, you know. You might have hurt yourself really badly.'

'I wonder why you never heard him when you searched in the stable earlier in the day. He must have miaowed like anything.'

'It's a very thick roof,' said Mr Jenks, 'and there isn't a chink, not even by the trap-door.'

'And now it's time for bed again,' announced Mrs Jenks. 'Is your mug empty?'

'It's empty,' I said, 'but Mr Tiggle's had a good share of it while Sally's been talking!'

'Do I *have* to go to bed again yet?' asked Sally,

yawning hugely. 'It's so nice and warm and comfortable sitting here.'

'It'll be just as warm in bed and much more comfortable. It's nearly time for the others, too.'

'Even heroes have to go to bed in the end, you know, Sally!' said Pat.

'Mm!' yawned Sally. 'But they don't always want to.'

That wasn't quite the end of the adventure. Next morning when we came down to breakfast there was a shining, new sixpence by Sally's plate, and, underneath it, a small card neatly printed in Pat's best script.

'What's this?' asked Sally picking it up.

We all watched her as she read it out aloud, slowly running her finger along beneath the words.

REWARD FOR GALLANTRY

For rescuing a dumb creature from a sad and certain end on the night of January 4th, this silver medal is awarded to:

SARAH MEREDITH MUNRO BROWNE

'That's me!' said Sally.

'Of course it is!'

'But who's the dumb creature?'

'Mr Tiggle.'

'Mr Tiggle!' said Sally scornfully. 'Mr Tiggle dumb! Why, you should just have heard the noise he made when I pushed that trap-door up!'

But the infant looked very pleased about the medal, all the same.

CHAPTER 15

Birding

JAN and I were lying on the hearth-rug, doing a variety of things in a lazy, after-tea way. He had one of his bird books out, and was idly turning the pages.

'That's a nice-looking little fellow,' I said. 'What is it?'

'Snow-bunting.'

'Ever seen one?'

'Well, I'm not certain,' said Jan. 'I rather think I did once, at the bottom of the cliffs above Angle Tarn. I didn't have time to stay then, but I've always intended to go back and look properly.'

'The book says it's "Six and a half inches long, a white bird with black on the back, tail, and wings. A winter visitor, seldom staying to breed except in the north of Scotland". It sounds nice; I wish I could see one.'

'We might go over to Angle Tarn some time, to look. Like to come?'

I stared at Jan in amazement, because I couldn't believe my ears. He is usually the *complete* solitary so far as bird-watching is concerned.

'I *say*!' I gasped. 'Do you really mean that?'

'Of course. Only don't get madly excited. We may see nothing except a couple of crows and a starling,' said Jan with a grin.

'I'm willing to risk it,' I declared firmly. 'When can we go?'

'What's planned for tomorrow?'

'Nothing specially, I think. Pat's been talking

mechanics all afternoon with Farmer Jenks, and they're going to take the lorry engine to pieces in the morning; they say it's been coughing for days. Oh, and I believe Kay's having a sock-wash; I saw her gathering up stacks of them from your room just after tea.'

'Right-ho, let's do it tomorrow, then. We'll take sandwiches, and get in a really long day.'

'*Grand!*' I said. 'If the weather's fine.'

'Oh, it will be. It's been like this ever since we came, and there's no sign of any change yet.'

Jan, of course, is the family optimist (and quite uncured by occasional surprises). But this time he was right, for we woke up to another brilliant morning, cold – though perhaps not quite so cold as it had been – and with a nice, vigorous breeze.

We got through breakfast and the after-breakfast chores in fine style, and then Jan and I dashed off to gather up our tackle. We put on masses of woollens, mitts and balaclavas and wind-jackets, because birdwatching in winter can be a frigid job. I suggested that oilskin capes might be a good thing, not because there was any sign of rain, but to use as one-man tents and wind-breaks if we had to sit watching for hours. Jan thought this quite a sound idea, so we rolled them up and strapped them on to our haversacks into which we'd already packed well-sharpened pencils, sketching-blocks, note-books, Jan's small *Observer's Book of Birds*, and (of course) large lunch packets.

Pat had already gone off with Farmer Jenks to the barn, and Kay and Sally were starting on the family sock-wash. This is almost a washing day in itself up here, as you can imagine when you realize that for walking we each wear two – and sometimes three – pairs at once, and that these, as well as our boots, generally finish the day by being completely caked with mud. By the time the mud has dried, the socks are so stiff that they stand up by themselves.

The only way to tackle the washing is to have about six buckets of soapy, warm water, and to take the socks through the lot. The last one just about sees them clear. We do them in the farm-yard, and then hang them in a long row from a clothes-line stretched between the pigsty and the stable.

'Sally's going to help'

Pat, who is heading for the navy, and knows all about 'Dressing ships over all' – whatever that may mean – says when we've got them up that it reads 'Splice the main brace', and promptly fetches out mugs of lemonade for us all, or cocoa if it's very cold. It is certainly a well-earned drink. Sock-wash is definitely a major operation.

So I felt quite guilty today when I saw the mountain of mud-caked socks that had been collected up.

'I say, Kay, I'd no idea there was such a pile. I think perhaps I'd better stay to do a share,' I suggested.

'Certainly not,' said Kay firmly. 'Sally's going to help, and it would be sheer waste of man-power to have three people on the job.'

It was awfully noble of her. I think she realized that the chance of being included in a bird-watching expedition wasn't one to be thrown away lightly.

'I'll do an extra share of darning to make up, then,' I offered, as we stood in the porch slinging bits of equipment on, and over, and about ourselves.

'Right-ho!' said Kay. 'Good birding!'

'Thanks awfully,' I said happily. 'I bet we come home with a lovely drawing of the Penelope Bird, or the last Dodo to be seen in Westmorland, maybe!'

Jan looked simply horrified. Birding is about the one thing he takes seriously and, as we clattered across the farm-yard, he gave me a lecture on the need to stick to facts in ornithology. It sounded quite impressive, and I humbly promised to do my best.

Before ten o'clock we were striding briskly down the Coniston road towards Tilberthwaite. It is quite a way beyond there, through Little Langdale, past Blea Tarn, up the head of the Langdale Valley, and finally by the steep gully of Rossett Gill to Angle Tarn; and winter days are so short. But the wind was behind us mostly, and we got up a good pace. I should think it must have been about midday when we topped the last steep col, and saw Angle Tarn in the high hollow in front of us. It is a wild and lonely region, especially in winter, with the cold, grey tarn lying under the sheer flank of Bowfell, and a wild confusion of broken crags and rocks all round.

'Funny how much less sunny and bright it looks up here, isn't it! I'd be ready to swear it's not half the

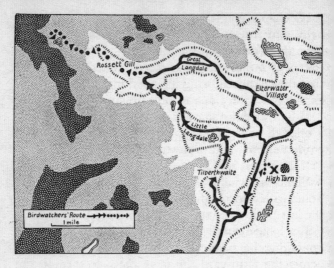

Birdwatchers' Route

day it was; but I expect it's just the general greyness of this place that makes the difference,' I said.

'Mm, I expect so,' Jan agreed. 'And of course there's always a good strong wind up that funnel of Rossett Gill. It's quite gusty, isn't it?'

'Yes, I'll be glad of a little shelter. Where are we going to cache ourselves?'

'I think the best thing to do will be to go as quietly as possible round the top of the tarn to the far side, and hide among the rocks there. It seems the likeliest place. And what do you say to eating a few sandwiches when we're settled?'

'*Agreed!*' I said emphatically. 'I feel that I could do with a little stoking up.'

We skirted the tarn, scrambling over and between

the boulders as quietly as we could, to avoid disturb-
ing any wild life that was about, and went to earth in
the end somewhere on the north-east side.

And going to earth is really what it felt like, for we
found the most perfect hide all ready made. It was
simply a tumble of rocks with a space in the middle,
just roomy enough for the two of us and our equipment. It even had a roof of sorts, so that the sky was

'*It's the* perfect *bird hide!*'

completely hidden; but on one side was a wide opening which gave us a perfect view of a corner of the
tarn, the rocky shore in front, and a section of the
sheer cliffs to the side.

'Goody,' said Jan. 'It's the *perfect* bird-hide. Nothing'd ever suspect there were humans inside.'

'Nice to be out of that wind, too; it was horribly
gusty.'

'There's not so much as a draught in here. What
do you think's in the sandwiches?'

F

We investigated them fairly thoroughly, then settled down for the afternoon's work.

'You've got to get yourself into a comfortable position right from the beginning,' said Jan. 'Then you don't need to wriggle. Put your note-book and things just handy, too. If you see a bird that you don't know jot down the most striking things about it, so that you can identify it later – and the same when you're drawing; don't try to make a picture with a background and all that. I don't think we'd better talk because we'd only disturb things.'

I took up what I thought was a correct bird-watching attitude, and settled down to watch. And really it was most extraordinarily interesting, even when nothing was happening, because you always felt that something would, in a moment. Indeed, by degrees, as the disturbance of our coming subsided, it *did* happen.

The first bird I saw was a little buff-coloured thing that flittered about on the boulders a dozen yards or so in front of us. I thought it was a Stone-chat, and I scribbled this down on my block underneath the three or four little sketches I'd made, so that I should remember to ask Jan later. It was while I was busy with this that he said, almost soundlessly:

'Hyacinth, look at that thing on the tarn – right out as far as you can see. It'll dive again in a second, I think.'

'Oh yes, I see!' I whispered. 'And there it goes. What a marvellous dive! What is it?'

'Golden Eye, I think: a sort of duck. I've seen it on some of the bigger lakes, but I didn't expect it up here. Isn't it a beauty?'

We watched it for some time, though it never came close in to us. We tried to draw it doing one of its really stunning dives, but it wasn't easy. After a time I saw something perched on the crags, big and black and motionless. I managed to draw Jan's attention to it.

'Raven, probably,' whispered Jan. 'Only it's not easy to tell when it's so still. Draw it if you get a chance, and if it moves. The light's not so good, is it?'

Maybe this description of an afternoon's watching sounds rather tame; but it really is most engrossing while it's on. I suppose it is the feeling of being unseen right in the middle of it all, so that you know that whatever happens, and whatever you see, is part of the creature's normal, everyday life.

Anyhow, I can tell you that we were both completely engrossed, so much so that I didn't even realize that my feet had gone soundly to sleep – and we neither of us noticed the weather.

Suddenly something white fluttered on to the rock in front – and it certainly wasn't a Snow-bunting!

CHAPTER 16

Then Blizzard

'Jan,' I said in amazement (and, I'm afraid, in a quite loud voice), 'it's snowing!'

'*Snowing!*' exclaimed Jan. 'It *can't* be. It was a perfect day when we started. Here, let's have a look!'

He scrambled out of the hide, stood up, looked round, and gave a whistle of astonishment.

'What a change! I shouldn't have said it could do it in the time.'

'We've been here quite a while,' I pointed out. 'Long enough for both my legs to go to sleep at any rate.'

'Can you waken them up quickly, then?' said Jan. 'Because I think we'd better be moving.'

I needn't tell you how agonizing it is to bring legs back to life quickly; but I screwed up my courage and did it, then set to work to collect up the tackle.

'A jolly good thing you suggested these oilskins,' said Jan rather grimly. 'We'll need them for their proper use. And I think we'd better put them on before we get out of the shelter. There's an awful squally wind blowing outside.'

So we packed away the books and sketching things, slung on the haversacks, fixed our balaclava helmets and mitts, put on the oilskin capes on top of everything else, and clamped them as firmly as possible.

But though we were jolly quick, the weather was quicker. By the time we stepped from the bird-hide the snow was coming down really hard so that the tarn and the cliffs were quite blotted out, and the first gust of wind that caught me almost laid me flat.

braced myself to withstand it – from whatever direction, because it was veering about most extraordinarily – and we started to battle our way round the head of the tarn.

And it *was* a fight, right from the word GO. You stumble over boulders there at the best of times, and this certainly wasn't the best. They were already covered with a loose, slippery layer of snow, the wind was coming from every direction in turn, and we couldn't see more than a yard or two ahead.

We clutched our oilskins round us, put our heads down, and tried to make our way towards the path that comes over Esk Hause to the top of Rossett Gill. But, with nothing but falling snow and grey mist in front, we could only guess at directions, and I'm afraid we went rather badly astray. It seemed ages before we did hit on the path, and I'm quite sure that we were much farther back towards the Hause than we should have been. Still, I was jolly glad to get on to it, because, though it is terribly rough, and the going wasn't much easier, we did at least know that we were heading in the right direction, and we generally discovered fairly quickly if we strayed from it, and didn't waste much time getting back.

But I've never before taken so long to cover such a short distance. By the time we reached Rossett Gill the light seemed almost to have gone, though we'd no idea whether that was because it was late afternoon, or whether it was just the smother of snow all round.

By now the blizzard had worked itself into a terrible frenzy. The full fury of it came rushing at us up the funnel of the Gill, and I thought for one moment that it would be impossible to take a single step down into it.

Rossett Gill is usually a jolly steep, rough scramble – and tremendous fun. Coming up had been more difficult than usual, because the boulders had been crusted with ice. Now the ice was covered with a gradually thickening layer of loose snow, the light had almost gone, and there was a furious, squally gale blowing from every direction in turn.

'Jan,' I gasped in horror, as we struggled down the first few yards, 'we'll *never* do it!'

'We've *got* to,' said Jan through clenched teeth. 'Come on, Hyacinth; it'll only get worse if we wait.'

Almost before he'd finished speaking he slipped off a boulder, and went slithering and bouncing down.

'Jan! Are you all right?' I called, clambering downwards as quickly as I could, for he was quite out of sight in the shrouding gloom.

'Mm, I think so.' (His voice, muffled and hollow, came from somewhere below.) 'Cut my hand a bit but nothing worse. That's a beastly rock, Hyacinth, so take care: sheer glass underneath the snow.'

That was the worst of our tumbles on the journey down Rossett Gill, but it certainly wasn't the last and, however carefully we went, we were constantly slipping about and landing in every position in turn – on our knees, or our seats, or our backs, or our heads, or even our faces. I suppose the snow did have its uses, because, as it got thicker and thicker, it softened the falls somewhat. I don't see how, otherwise, we could have escaped with nothing more serious than odd cuts and bruises and torn clothes.

But it was terrifying; and it seemed endless. I don't think I've ever been so near to exhaustion as I was when we reached the bottom of the Gill. We knew

that we had got there, because the ground flattens
out into the wild stretch of the upper Langdale
Valley, but it was by this time completely dark, and
terribly difficult to guess directions.

'Whichever way *is* it, Jan?' I said. 'It's hopeless
trying to find the path; there's not a sign of it under
this snow.'

Went ahead as planned

'I know. I wish to goodness we'd a compass. Look,
Hyacinth! Isn't this a wall? D'you think it might be
the sheep-fold, the one right up at the valley head?
If it is we'll keep it on our right hands, and the next
thing we'll have to look out for is the crossing over
the ghyll that comes down from the Stake Pass.'

It was the sheep-fold. We proved that by working
our way all round it. Then when we got back to our
starting-point (we could see our own footprints) we
went ahead as we'd planned.

At least, we thought we did, but in fact we were

simply wandering in a maze, and, after a time, I began to suspect that we were also wandering in circles.

'Jan!' I gasped. 'Aren't those our footprints in front?'

'Golly,' said Jan. 'I believe they are! This one just fits, and it's got all the nail marks.'

'In fact,' I said bitterly, 'if we go a bit farther we'll probably reach the sheep-fold again.'

We did. It lay quite correctly on our right hand, as before.

'It's no use,' I panted. 'We're just going round and round in circles, and I don't believe I can take another step.'

'Yes you can, Hyacinth,' said Jan, grim and determined. 'Come on. We'll manage this time. Look, let's verge away from our last time's footprints when they begin to curve. If we leave them well on our right-hand side we'll surely be going in a straight line.'

It sounded a good plan, and we certainly seemed to be walking straight ahead. In fact we struggled on like that for quite a long time, though it didn't appear to be getting us anywhere. We had been walking mechanically, just battling ahead; then I glanced down.

'Jan!' I exclaimed in horror. 'We're on our own tracks again!'

'I know,' said Jan. 'I noticed them about two minutes ago. We've done a bigger circle this time, that's all. We'll be reaching the sheep-fold again at any moment.'

We did, and I could have sat down and wept – if only there had been something less cold and damp than snow on which to sit.

'What *can* we do?' I said. 'It's this wind, and the awful gloom, and the choking snow, and –'

'Try again: there's nothing else possible. I suppose we finished the sandwiches?'

'Scopped the lot!' I said bitterly, using one of Mr Jenks' pet expressions.

I think that if I had been alone I should just have decided to lie down in the snow and die. But that isn't really the sort of thing you can do in pairs so, once again, though I thought that every step would be my last, I followed Jan in what we felt must, surely, be the right direction.

Just about that time the most extraordinary thing happened. For a few minutes the wind dropped completely. Before, it had been coming from every direction in turn, and we'd braced ourselves against its buffetings, and struggled headlong into it. Suddenly it left us. We heard it go tearing away towards the high crags, screaming ferociously. Then it was gone, and we were left gasping for air among the smothering flakes that fell twice as heavily.

All round us, beyond the snow, was nothing but darkness, silence, and a most uncanny stillness. My feet felt like lead as I struggled to lift them. I thought that probably we'd have to go on like this, plodding aimlessly through a veiled world, for the rest of our lives.

Jan stopped.

'What is it?' I said dully.

'Listen, Hyacinth! Can you hear?'

I did listen, and heard the first encouraging sound for hours – a faint, *very* faint, call that came in a funny, muffled way through the blanketing darkness.

'It's someone calling!' said Jan excitedly. 'I think they must be looking for us!'

'If they are,' I said, feeling more completely weary than I'd ever done in my life before, 'I think I'll just stand here and let them find me. D'you think you could possibly call back?'

'Curlwee, curlwee, curlwee!'

Jan gave the family bird call that they could not possibly fail to recognize. And I believe I even found the energy to join in the last one.

There was really quite a lot more to that day – because we were still miles from home, with no way of getting there except on foot, and the snow was falling faster than ever. But I'm glad to say that I don't remember much about it.

I have a sort of hazy recollection of calls getting closer and closer, and of three rather shapeless figures – which proved to be Mr Jenks, Kay, and Pat – plodding towards us out of the awful grey blanket.

I can remember, too, the marvellous sight of a thermos being pulled from a haversack, and the wonderful glow that spread all over me as the hot coffee went down my gullet. I'd have said before, that lemonade was easily my favourite drink, or possibly cocoa in winter, or cider-cup at parties. But that day I gave top place to piping hot coffee, though my teeth were chattering so much that they rattled against the cup, and the coffee was so hot that it scalded my tongue.

I have only the faintest memory of the long trek home. I believe that I did it more than half asleep, with Kay and Mr Jenks, one on either side, to bolster me up; and I have a vague recollection of Jan

Three rather shapeless figures

and Pat plodding along side by side, somewhere ahead.

My last memory of the day is of the four of us sprawling in front of a huge, log fire, in pyjamas and dressing-gowns, after we'd had hot baths and a good hot meal, feeling gloriously warm and lazy, and far too weary to make the effort to get upstairs to bed.

We learnt a bit more then about all that had happened at High Tarn during the day; of how Farmer Jenks, standing in the farm-yard at mid-morning, and sniffing the wind, had prophesied a weather change – to everybody's great surprise.

'He was right, of course,' said Kay. 'In less than an hour there was a most awful blizzard raging, and we had to take down the line of socks in a fearful hurry. It was a good thing that Pat mentioned you two at dinner.'

'Why, what did he say?'

'Oh, something about the blizzard damping your style, and that it was lucky you'd only gone as far as Tarn Hows.'

'Tarn Hows!' I exclaimed. 'My goodness! Didn't you know where we were?'

'Sally did. She said you hadn't only gone to Tarn Hows; you'd gone up Langdale and Rossett Gill to Angle Tarn.'

'And stuck to her guns, too,' declared Farmer Jenks who had just come in, 'when we weren't for believing her.'

'My goodness!' I said again, thinking how easily we might still have been plodding endlessly through that awful greyness. 'Wouldn't it have been *ghastly* for us if she hadn't?'

'It would indeed. But she was dead certain of it, and we decided on a search-party right away. And that was no picnic, either, even when we'd some idea of where you were. We weren't certain we'd ever make it.'

'It must have been grim, trekking all that way over to Langdale, and then up the valley.'

'It was,' said Kay, 'especially as we didn't know which route you'd take, so we had to go separately. Farmer Jenks went by Tilberthwaite and Little Langdale, and Pat and I by Elterwater and through Chapel Stile. And we had to divide at the old and new roads. I must say I was thankful when we all linked up again at the Old Hotel – though I did think that

Mr Jenks was a snow man, sheltering in a corner by the barn. He'd even got snow on his eyebrows.'

'Goodness!' I said for the third time, and very fervently. 'It's votes of thanks to all three of you from Jan and me.'

'And to the infant, too, in the morning,' declared Jan.

'That's so. And what about learning a bit of weather forecasting? Bird-watching's all right, but there are other things it's as well to know about, too,' said Farmer Jenks dryly.

'Mm!' admitted Jan. 'I s'pose there are.' Which – for Jan – sounded almost humble.

Mrs Jenks came in at that moment to announce that we could have five minutes more, then it was bed for the lot of us. Jan said in that case he'd use the time to eat another biscuit. It seemed to me a good plan, and I remember that I chose the biggest. Which goes to prove, I suppose, that we were then well on the way to recovery.

CHAPTER 17

A Deepening Depression

WE woke up on the morning after our rescue to find that the blizzard was still raging, and that a completely new set of mountains had grown up around us overnight. They were snow mountains.

There was a mighty one that reached almost to the top of the boys' bedroom window. It was built of snow whipped from the windward side of the knoll, and dropped in the slight hollow between that and the farm-house. There were others half-way up the windows downstairs; and the pantry window – which is very close to the ground – was completely screened, so that the gloom never lifted in there all day.

'Just right for a smash-and-grab raid,' Jan suggested, as we cleared after breakfast. I needn't say that at that moment none of us felt inclined to act on the suggestion.

Mr Jenks opened the front door with difficulty at about eight-thirty, just as a rather grey daylight first appeared; and but for the fact that it opened into the porch I don't think he'd have managed it at all. He certainly had a bit of a struggle until Pat and Jan weighed in with a shoulder each. The snow had piled up even inside the porch to the height of the key-hole. They swept it back like a snow-plough, and got the door ajar.

Inside the porch it was fairly sheltered. Jan blithely scrambled up on to the top of the snow mound, and immediately the full force of the wind caught him.

He overbalanced, and came tumbling back twice as quickly as he'd gone up.

Outside, the air seemed thick, though we couldn't really tell whether it was still snowing heavily, or whether it was simply being blown about by the wind, which was certainly buffeting and squalling and shrieking like a pack of hobgoblins. Some places in the teeth of the gale had been whipped almost clear. In others the snow was piled up many feet deep. It sloped in great, smooth curves from the farm-yard almost to the roof of the barn. There were wonderful cornices and overhangs along the top of the walls and the pigsty; and, from all the crests, great plumes of snow were blowing like smoke.

'Not be much getting about today,' said Farmer Jenks. 'Nor for a few days to come, I guess.'

'What about the sheep on Black Fell?' I asked. 'Will they be all right?'

'Aye, if they sensed that it was coming, and made their way down into the lower meadows. I'd like to slip down there, and take a look at them.'

'I'll come with you, shall I?' said Pat promptly.

'Put on oilskins, then, and your balaclava helmet too. You'll find you can breathe better in this with your nose covered.'

Jan and I begged to go too, but Mr Jenks was firm.

'Two of us is enough. It's no picnic being out in this. Tell you what you can do, though. Have a shot at clearing some of that snow away from the door, and see if you can make a path of sorts across to the barn.'

'You'll need to wear your gaberdines,' said Mrs Jenks, who had just come through from the kitchen, 'and your sou'westers and Wellingtons, or you'll be soaked through in five minutes.'

Mr Jenks was quite right about it not being a picnic outside. He and Pat ploughed their way across the snowdrifts to the farm gate, and turned there into the teeth of the wind, so that, for a few seconds, we thought they would never get farther. When they had

Turned our attention to our battle with the blizzard

disappeared, Jan and I turned our attention to our own battle with the blizzard. And it *was* a tussle, I can tell you, with a wind that cut like a knife, and blew streams of stinging wet snow into our eyes to blind us. We had got two big spades, as big as boiler shovels, and a stiff yard brush; but, muffled up in gaberdines and sou'westers and scarves and Wellingtons, it wasn't easy to use them, and, for a time, we thought that new snow was being piled up more quickly than we could move it.

But it really was good fun, and we worked like

navvies, so that when Mr Jenks and Pat came struggling uphill into the farm-yard we'd got a sort of
rough and ready channel cut through from the door
of the farm-house to the barn. We built up the
snow as high as we could on the windward side,
hoping that the fresh snow would either pile up
outside that, or else blow right over the top of the
path.

'That's quite a nice job you've made of it,' said
Farmer Jenks approvingly, drawing his breath in
great gulps, as though he'd not been able to snatch
any air lower down.

'How are things in the meadow?' asked Jan.

'Pretty bad, but might be worse.'

'Have the sheep from Black Fell got down?'

'Most of them, I think. They've huddled themselves along the walls for shelter, and behind the
knolls and in the clumps of fir trees. Look a bit miserable, but they'll come to no harm there.'

'But suppose they get snowed up?'

'Likely they will, but it won't hurt them for a time,
and we'll know where to dig for them later. Sometimes the snow comes unexpectedly, and they get
caught on the fells and buried there. We can't reach
them at first, and later we don't know where to dig
for them. They may be anywhere for miles around,
and it's then that we lose so many.'

'Whatever'll they find to eat?' I asked. 'They
can't scratch through all this snow to the turf underneath, can they?'

'Only where it's been blown thin,' said Mr Jenks.
'They'll be hungry, no doubt; and we'll have to get
fodder down to them as soon as the blizzard lets up.

But we can't do it yet – and we'd better all get indoors, or we'll be turning into snowmen standing
here.'

We were glad to get back inside after our struggles
and our buffetings. It was certainly an indoor day,
and we all found it quite fun at first to watch the
snow mounting higher and higher, to have the light
on at noon, and to lounge by the fire, reading and
chatting.

But we are not really an indoor family, and that
sort of life doesn't go on being fun for long. Even
meals become less interesting when you don't have a
chance to get really ravenous in between; and by
early afternoon on the second storm-bound day,
tempers were beginning to fray a bit.

Pat snapped at me quite viciously when I answered a question of his rather absent-mindedly. I
was absolutely wrapped up in Hippo at that moment,
so I don't know what else he could have expected.
But I suppose I ought not to have hurled a book at
his head. It caught him a stinging blow, just behind
the right ear.

But we really touched low at about two-thirty
when – to all our amazement – Sally punched Jan
on the nose. I don't think that, on this occasion, he
was really to blame; and I don't believe the infant
meant to do it. It was just one of those things that
happen.

She was painting, kneeling on a stool by the table.
Jan, who said that he could feel his muscles stiffening
up from not being used, was doing some vigorous
limbering exercises in one corner. They were rather
too vigorous for that space, and suddenly he jogged

the table with his knee. Sally's jam-jar of water toppled over and, before she could snatch it away, the painting was submerged.

It was a sea scene, very wet looking, so I don't think a little more water did any harm. But I suppose it came as a shock to Sally, and she punched with fury.

Felt his nose with care

We were absolutely startled, Jan worse than anyone. He sat on the floor where he'd landed, and felt his nose with care. I think he wondered whether she'd broken it. Sally flapped her watery picture, and looked ready to burst into tears.

'What we need,' said Pat firmly, 'is a bad-weather activity. Kay, d'you remember a climbing book I lent you last term?'

'Yes, but I *did* give it back to you, I'm sure,' said Kay, rather sharply for her.

'Of course you did,' Pat said hurriedly, feeling, I suppose, that we *had* got into a low state if Kay showed signs of crossness. 'But do you remember, in that, the way they used to practise climbing and keep in form on off-weather days?'

'Oh yes,' said Kay, more mildly. 'At one of those climbing places at Wasdale Head. They did indoor climbs in a billiard-room didn't they?'

'Mm!' said Pat. 'And I was thinking we might do the same thing here, in the barn.'

The crisis seemed to be passing, and everyone was interested. Sally had forgotten her water-logged picture, and Jan his battered nose.

'Oh, *do* let's,' I said eagerly. 'I've got the Blood-stained Hippo into the most awful jam, and I can't think *how* to get him out. I'd rather like to leave him there a bit.'

The depression was definitely lifting.

CHAPTER 18

Indoor Activities

WE dashed off to the kitchen to tell Mrs Jenks that we would be in the barn for the rest of the afternoon.

'Please will you let us know when it's tea-time?' asked Jan.

'Of course I will,' said Mrs Jenks. 'But it wants more than two hours to that yet, so if you're hungry you'd better put a few biscuits in your pockets.'

'No thank you,' said Kay firmly. 'We've been eating too much, and doing too little. It's bad for the tempers – that's the trouble. We're going to work a bit of it off now.'

'Right you are, then,' said Mrs Jenks. 'I'll ring the cow bell from the front door when tea's ready. You'll hear that for certain.'

It was only about ten yards across the farm-yard to the barn, but today it seemed almost as inaccessible as the North Pole. We hugged our oilskins round us, opened the door as little as possible to wriggle through, then made a dash for it. There was still a remnant of the path which Jan and I had made.

Inside the barn we shook ourselves as dogs do when they've been swimming, and deposited quite a mound of snow on the stone floor.

'I say!' I exclaimed. 'What a place for "Pirates"!'

'Goodness, yes!' agreed Kay. 'I never thought of it before.'

'What's "Pirates"?' Pat asked.

'A game we play in the gym – at end of term, or

when Sorbo's feeling benign. You space out evenly, then dash round and round trying to catch the one in front, but without stepping on the ground at all.'

'What do you step on to, then?'

'Oh, anything you can find,' said Kay. 'In the gym we travel along the wall bars and over the horse and box and along the forms, and swing by the ropes on to the window-ledges, or anything handy.'

'*Sounds* all right,' said Jan in a surprised voice. I suppose he didn't imagine such good things going on in girls' schools.

'It's jolly fine,' I declared. 'I vote we try it. We'd only need to move a thing or two.'

So we did a bit of shifting about of objects till we'd got a possible route. Beginning along the short east wall it went across the top of the haystack; from the end, which was pretty high, you climbed on to one of the rafters, swung down on to the wood-pile, and did the rest of the long south side via a wheelbarrow, a window-ledge, and the big, wooden hay-sledge. That brought you to the west side, a short one again but a bit of a corker, because the only footholds were a coil of rope, the chimney part – where you either balanced across some old fire-dogs on the hearth (very wobbly) or wriggled along the mantelpiece (very narrow) – and finally a broken, three-legged stool, which wasn't over steady.

Then came the long north side, where there was a pile of junk (cart-wheels and such), a long, wooden form, a sheep-pen hurdle, and an old water butt upended. That brought you to the last obstacle of all, the barn door itself. You swung on to it from the water-butt, did a finger traverse of the top, and dropped once again on to the haystack at its lower end.

It seemed a jolly good round. We spaced ourselves out – Sally on the hay, Jan in the wheelbarrow, Kay on top of the coil of rope, me on the junk-pile, and Pat on the water-butt.

'Remember that you drop out into the middle if you're touched, or if you touch the floor even the teeniest bit,' said Kay. 'Are you all ready? Then one – two – three – GO!'

That first round Pat and Jan both did themselves

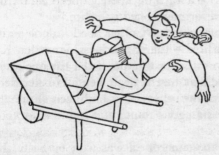

I fell out of the wheelbarrow

in by aiming too much at speed. Jan managed the fireplace at a colossal rate, but missed the stool at the far end by inches. Pat tried to get from the hayrick on to the beam and down on to the wood-pile all in one swing, lost his balance, and slithered on to the floor. I caught Sally, then, next moment, fell out of the wheelbarrow. So Kay, who'd been going round very neatly and carefully, was the winner.

'It's steadiness does it,' said Pat, 'not speed. Come on, let's try again.'

This time we went to the other extreme, jumped primly from one obstacle to the next, weighed up carefully the amount of spring needed, and followed each other round in a stately sort of procession, evenly spaced. We'd forgotten all about the catching part, and were concentrating on not falling off. Then Pat suddenly did a spurt, caught up Sally, Jan, and Kay, and gave me such a fright that I tumbled off the haystack – the easiest bit. That, of course, left Pat the winner.

'Come on,' said Jan enthusiastically, 'another round. It's a rattling good game. Can't think why you've never mentioned it before.'

'Because we don't often need indoor activities in Westmorland – thank goodness!' retorted Kay.

Jan won the next game, and I the one after. Then Kay and Pat had a dead heat. We decided it was that, after the others of us had been eliminated, and they two had gone round and round a dozen times or so.

The last game of all was won by Sally. Kay and Pat and I all dropped on to the floor in the first half-minute. Jan's attention was distracted on the hayrick by something he said was a rat; and, while he was investigating, the infant shot along the form, swung across the door, and hurled herself over the hayrick to grab him so violently that they both rolled together off the end.

That just about left us exhausted. We sat about, to cool down and to get our second winds.

'You know,' said Pat, 'we really could do here what they did in the billiard-room at Wasdale Head.'

'You mean indoor climbing?'

'Mm! Just look at the way that wall slopes back, and all those knobbly bits for foot and hand-holds.'

'And we could do belays with the rope, round the rafters and so on, like Bill Wetherby showed us in summer.'

'Let's each work out a climb, and then demonstrate in turn. Anyone want any particular spot?'

'Bags I the end rafter!' said Jan.

'I'd like that sloping bit,' said Kay. 'I do believe there are foot and hand-holes to the very top.'

'I'd like the sheer north wall,' I said. 'North walls are always pretty grim – in climbing books at any rate.'

Sally said she'd climb the door, and Pat thought he'd investigate the chimney – which sounded pretty professional.

We took our second winds, and set to work with enthusiasm.

Jan was soon swinging gaily from his rafter, doing hand traverses. He is good with his arms, partly because he's done lots of tree-climbing when bird-watching. Sally had a grand time on the barn door, climbing up and down and across it in every imaginable way. I believe that once when I glanced across she was hanging by the feet, head downwards, from the top bar.

Kay's wall needed mostly good footwork and balance. It was the sort of thing (on a small scale, of course) that you often get in real rock-climbing when you have to negotiate a bulge that simply hangs over space.

'Mine's a corker,' I said, after I'd had one or two shots at it. 'I guess I'll never reach the top.'

'There seem some good bits. I can see a whole set of foot-holds – almost like a ladder.'

'I know, but then they stop; and the only ones for the top half are right over at the other end.'

'That's the whole art of climbing sheer rock-faces, isn't it?' said Pat. 'Making the different sections fit together.'

He was standing in the open hearth, looking upwards thoughtfully.

'What's wrong with your chimney?' I asked. 'Isn't that climbable, either?'

'Oh yes, I think so; but it's a bit Alpine. All the ledges are coated thick with frozen snow. No use trying in these rubbers. I think I'll dash across for my boots.'

He was back in half a minute, dangling his nailed boots in one hand, and a hatchet in the other.

'Whatever –?' exclaimed Kay.

'Ice-axe, or anyhow the nearest I could get to one. Might as well do the thing professionally,' explained Pat. He tugged on his boots, and soon they were the last that was to be seen of him as he disappeared up the chimney.

When we felt that we'd done all we could on our own sections we joined forces for a guided climb, Kay leading, up her west wall. From there we swung on to Jan's rafter for a hand traverse along it – which brought us, of course, to the top of my great north wall.

And that rafter was the only way in which we ever did reach the top. I'd got once to a point three-quarters of the way up, but there I'd stuck completely, unable to budge up or down. Pat mustered a

'Mountain Rescue Squad'; he stood on the upturned water-butt, with the others standing by to act as stretcher-bearers if needed, and I scrambled down via his shoulders. We decided that it was quite impossible to do the complete climb from top to bottom, and we labelled it the 'North, or Indomitable, Face'.

Ascent (with ice-axe) of Jackdaw chimney

Farmer Jenks looked in – for his tool-bag, he said, but I think that he just wanted to see the fun.

'Ought to write all these climbs up, for the journal of the "Fell and Rock",' he chuckled.

'*That's* an idea!' I said enthusiastically (for I can never resist a suggestion to write things down). 'There's an old exercise book in the pocket of my oilskin. Anyone got a pencil?'

Jan produced a ghastly stump of one from among

the other oddments in his pocket; and at intervals after that I scribbled down climbing notes and directions, so that we finished up with quite a professional 'Handbook of First Ascents and Pioneer Routes'. There was the 'Guideless Ascent (with ice-axe) of Jackdaw Chimney', so-called after the dead bird Pat found there on a ledge, the 'West Wall Bulge and Overhang', leading to the 'Rafter Col', and the 'Hand Traverse (by Rafter Route) to the top of the Indomitable Face', and so on.

We also finished with a fair number of cuts and bruises. I had a lump the size of a pigeon's egg on my head, where I had come up against a hanging buttress; and Pat scraped a large area of skin from his left shin when he fell half the length of my old Indomitable.

But such things, of course, are all in the climbing game.

CHAPTER 19

Tracks in the Snow

THAT blizzard went on for three whole days, then exactly what we'd hoped for happened, and half-way between tea and bedtime we realized that the wind was no longer tearing and howling like a pack of hobgoblins round the chimneys.

About seven o'clock Mr Jenks went to the front door, opened it wide, and sniffed hard, as he always does when there is any weather to smell. Outside it was jet black, except for a blaze of stars. There wasn't a sound, or a breath of wind.

'Well, that's the end of the snowfall for the present, I guess,' he said. 'And it'll freeze hard to-night.'

We knew that he would be right; he always is with weather, and anyhow we could feel the iciness creeping in from outside.

'Shut that door, then, do,' said Mrs Jenks. 'Or you'll have us frozen stiff as we sit here. Is the big oil-stove full, I wonder? We'd better leave it burning in the bathroom tonight, or we'll likely find all the pipes frozen up in the morning.'

It is strange how grown-ups see the gloomy side of such matters as frost. I'd thought straight away of all the fun we'd have in the snow tomorrow; and I guess that the others had thought of this, too.

I hoped like anything that there wouldn't be another quick change, and that we wouldn't get up tomorrow to find the wind howling like hobgoblins again, whipping up damp snow from one place, piling it in another, and plastering your face and stinging your eyes if you had to be outside.

It must have weighed quite a lot on my mind, because I believe I even woke up in the night. But when I opened one eye I could see about a million stars shining in a completely inky sky; so I went to sleep again straight away, and had some jolly good dreams.

And next day was even better than the dreams, in fact just about perfect. It didn't come light, of course, till after we'd finished breakfast, but when it did arrive it was the sort of day I'd hoped for, with blue sky, brilliant sun, and masses of white snow, crisp and sparkling, that made us impatient to get outside.

Mr Jenks was just as pleased at the change as we were.

'Be able to get some fodder down to the sheep,' he said, looking at the frozen snow with satisfaction. 'And none too soon, either.'

'How'll you take it—'

'In the hay-sledge – and I'll need a working party to help.'

'We'll be with you in ten minutes,' said Pat, beginning to stack breakfast things together as quickly as he could.

We cleared at a great rate – which isn't, of course, always the quickest way of getting through chores. Fortunately Pat managed to field the saucer that slithered out of Sally's fingers, and Kay unearthed the three teaspoons that Jan accidentally threw away with the scraps into the pig-bin; so, in the end, there were no losses. Then we dashed across to the barn where Mr Jenks was already loading up with bales of hay and turnips.

The sledge is a huge one, about the size of a farm cart, and with the same sort of shafts. It is used oftenest in summer, with Bobbin harnessed to it, to bring in the hay crop, or dead bracken for bedding, from the steep, rocky meadows where an ordinary wheeled cart would be useless. All fell farms have these wooden sledges.

But Mr Jenks wasn't harnessing Bobbin today, because he'd have floundered helplessly in the snow-drifts. Instead he enrolled us as a sort of human dogteam to drag it down.

As a matter of fact it wasn't so much dragging as holding it back that was the problem. The track from the farm-yard slopes terrifically, and the sledge would have careered down quite happily on its own – though it certainly wouldn't have landed in the right place.

Mr Jenks fixed a rope across the shafts, and another one loosely across the back. Pat went in front and used the first rope to steer, while Mr Jenks, Kay, Jan, and I hung on to the one at the back to keep it under control. We had to tug back quite hard occasionally.

It must have been a funny sight – the sledge doing the pulling, the sledge team hanging on behind – but the sheep didn't seem to mind. In fact they gave us a great welcome. I've never before seen sheep take much interest in people, except some of the ewes, which get very wary at lambing time. But these came trotting briskly to meet us, and they were at the hay before we'd unloaded. I guess they were jolly hungry.

I know that I should have been if I'd had nothing to eat since the blizzard began.

We scattered the turnips on top of the frozen snow, and then after Mr Jenks had looked round to see that the sheep were all right, we tugged the sledge back to the farm-yard. This time it was a case of everyone pulling, and we were jolly glad that it was not still loaded.

'Couldn't we use this as a toboggan?' I suggested.

'If we put planks of wood across to sit on?'

'Mm,' said Pat, 'family size! We'd get all five of us on.'

'And the dogs.'

'And Mr Tiggle.'

'And Louisa the sow – if she'd come.'

'*And* me and Mrs Jenks, too,' chuckled Mr Jenks. 'And a nice jumble we'd all be in if we took a toss!'

'It does seem a pity to churn up all this nice, white, frosty surface, doesn't it?' I said as we rounded the gate into the farm-yard. 'You can see the furrows the sledge has made right down to the meadow, and all our footprints.'

'In fact,' said Pat, 'you can see everything that's happened hereabouts this morning. There's where Sally and Mr Tiggle went across to the intak for the eggs, and this is where we all rushed across to the barn.'

'Footsteps of all sizes! Those biggest are Mr Jenks' gum-boots.'

'Gosh, aren't they monsters!'

'Pat's aren't much smaller,' declared Mr Jenks.

'Sally turns her toes in!' scoffed Jan.

'I don't care,' said Sally, who had come out with crumbs for the birds. 'So does Mr Tiggle.'

'It's Hyacinth who ought to be nosing about among these. It'd be practice for when she comes to the footprint clues in the "Hippo".'

'*Are* there footprint clues?'

'*Sally turns her toes in!*'

'Sure to be,' said Pat, 'in a thriller. Hoy, Hyacinth, what are these?'

'Birds!' I said, much relieved that he'd dropped on something so simple.

'Too vague,' protested Pat. 'You ought to say what sort.'

'Oh goodness! We-ll, not eagle's, certainly. Might be a robin's,' I suggested, examining the little three-pronged prints.

'These are rabbits, aren't they?' said Jan. 'You

can see where they've lolloped all round here; two
paws together, and two on the slant.'

'This one's the father and mother of all rabbits,
then,' said Kay. 'It's three times as big as the rest!'

'That's not rabbit,' declared Mr Jenks.

'It's one of the dogs, isn't it?' asked Pat.

'No.'

'What is it then?'

'Fox.'

'A fox! How thrilling! How d'you know?'

'Well, it's rather like a dog's really,' said Mr Jenks.
'So Pat's wasn't a bad guess; smaller than a sheep-
dog's, though.'

'Where's it gone?'

'Not into the intak, let's hope, or it'd be after the
hens.'

'No,' said Jan. 'Look, it went over the wall here,
and you can see prints going down towards the
copse. It's heading for Tarn Hows, I should say.'

'How exciting. *Do* let's track it!' I suggested.

So Pat, Kay, Jan, and I scrambled over the wall,
and set off in a bunch towards the fir copse.

'Keep to one side of the actual footprints, not right
on the line of them,' said Pat as we lolloped along.
'Then if we lose the track and have to come back to
pick it up again it isn't all churned up.'

'Not much chance of losing these, is there? They're
as clear as a die on this smooth, crisp snow. You can
see them perfectly, right on into the copse.'

'Wait till we get into the trees, though, where the
snow's thinner, or where the ground's broken and
there are boulders. They won't be so plain then.'

We followed the prints into the fir copse, slowing

down to a walking pace because of the more difficult going, and because the tracks were certainly not so easy to follow. Under a tall spruce we came upon a wild confusion of feathers, palish grey and buff.

'It's a wood-pigeon,' exclaimed Jan angrily. 'The old killer!'

'Perhaps he didn't kill it,' I suggested hopefully. 'Perhaps the pigeon got away.'

'With a wing torn off!' snorted Jan. 'Not likely!'

'Lucky Farmer Jenks' hens were safely fastened up last night,' said Pat. 'Look, he's gone on again this way.'

We followed the tracks across the rough, rocky land below the copse, over the Tarn Hows road (we could see where his tail had brushed away the snow as he skimmed the walls), and along as far as Tarn Hows itself. There, amid a whole medley of rabbit tracks, that criss-crossed and diverged in all directions, we lost them.

It was a good spot. The sun was shining from a clear, blue sky, we were in the middle of a perfect bowl of sparkling fells, and the tarn was just below us. We sat down to cool on a fallen tree, brushing it clear first; even the crispest snow, when sat on, soon becomes very damp.

'Listen!' said Kay. 'What's that?'

We sat in silence for a moment, stretching our ears; and heard, from far off, the deep-throated sounds of baying.

'Hounds, begorrah!' exclaimed Pat.

'They're not – hunting, are they?' I gasped, thinking of the little wild tawny creature that was lost from us somewhere among these wooded crags.

'Not in this weather,' said Pat. 'They'll be walking them, I expect, for exercise. They'll have been cooped up for days in the kennels.'

'Thank goodness! It'd have been awful if he'd got caught, and they had killed him, wouldn't it?'

'He killed the wood-pigeon,' Jan said. 'And he robs their nests.'

'I know,' I admitted. 'I suppose he did that because he was hungry. It's horrid, though, to think of hunting and killing just for the fun of it.'

'They don't so much here, do they?' Pat pointed out. 'They hunt to keep down the numbers, or else they'd be an awful pest to the farmers. This chap would have had one or two of Farmer Jenks' hens if they hadn't been locked up safely; and they're a menace at lambing time.'

'And it's a jolly strenuous sort of hunting, too,' interrupted Jan, 'because they've got to do all the following on foot, right up among the crags. No use thinking you can trot round comfortably on horseback here.'

'I know all that,' I said. 'And I know it's difficult to decide what's right. But if they *have* to do it I wish they'd kill them in a different way. Couldn't they shoot them instead of letting them be torn to pieces by a pack of hounds?'

'They do have shoots, sometimes, don't they?' said Kay. 'When there are so many that they really become a menace.'

'In fact,' said Pat, 'what Hyacinth objects to is all the gore. But I bet there's any amount of that in her old "Blood-stained Hippo".'

'That's different,' I said, rather hotly. 'Hippo's

just a story. Besides, it's only the wicked who die in it.
I'm taking jolly good care that right triumphs in the
end.'

'Good!' scoffed Pat. 'I hope you've got the
moral written in words of one syllable in the last para-
graph.'

'Look!' exclaimed Kay. 'There they are. Just
going up that brow on the mountain road.'

We all looked where she pointed, and saw what I
must admit was a very lovely sight – the pink-coated
huntsman striding up the steep road, with a dozen or
so of the small, palish hounds loping along beside him.

'They've got the terriers with them, too. Look, two
little brown fellows.'

'One has a hound leashed to it, d'you see? And
some of the hounds are chained together in pairs.
Why's that?'

'Training them,' explained Pat. 'They chain the
young ones to the older animals.'

'Funny that little terrier chap looks with a hulking
hound in tow! He's got the upper hand, though.'

We watched them over the series of brows on the
road, going farther and farther away from us. At the
nearest point the yelping and yapping was almost
ear-splitting. It was better heard more distantly, and
we sat in silence for a long time listening to the deep-
throated baying. At its farthest point it seemed like
far-distant music.

'Look!' I exclaimed suddenly. 'What's that – at
the other side of the tarn – high up?'

A tawny-coated creature ran swiftly across the
snow, with the low, crouching run of a dog rounding
up sheep.

'Sheep-dog,' said Kay.

''Tisn't,' said Pat. 'It's the fox!'

'Gracious!' I cried in horror. 'He's heading straight for the mountain road! He's going to run right into the pack of hounds, and they'll have him, I guess, even if they're *not* out hunting.'

'Don't you worry,' said Pat comfortably. 'Old Rufus can look after himself better than that. He'd

Stood for about five seconds

scent them a mile off, easily. He's just rounding the slope and heading for those woods, I should think.'

'Oh, I *hope* so. Isn't he beautiful!'

He went like a streak of tawny red across the glistening white snow, with a big brush of tail flying behind. Then he leapt on to a snow-covered wall, stood for about five seconds to give us a perfect view, slid down the other side, and was lost to sight.

'Time we went, too.' Kay got up rather stiffly.

'This sun's nice, but it isn't really the day for sitting about. My circulation's just about at a standstill, I think.'

'Must be getting on towards dinner-time, too,' said Pat; which brought Jan and me to our feet at once.

We went back along the edge of the tarn, through the trees and over the ladder to the road. Then, while the others climbed the wall at the far side, I lingered for a while, peering along the road to make sure that the fox wasn't heading that way. There seemed no sign; but I wished that the brows and bends didn't obstruct the view so much.

'Good luck, Rufus!' I said. 'Only kill things when you're hungry. And *do* keep away from Farmer Jenks' hen huts!'

Then I scrambled over the wall and dashed to catch the others up. They'd got on at a good pace; I expect because they knew that dinner was somewhere ahead.

CHAPTER 20

Last Day

WE woke to a day that might almost have been spring. Even though the sun had not yet really risen we knew that the iciness had somehow lost its grip overnight, and the thaw had begun. By mid-morning it was brilliant. There was the sound of dripping water everywhere and, now and again, a dull plop as the layers of snow on the roof gradually folded themselves up and slipped over the edge. The birds were singing with all their might. They evidently thought well of the day; and so might we have done, too, but for the fact that it was the last one of the holidays.

There was much to do – first and foremost, of course, the packing; and we set to work immediately after breakfast. Kay was in charge, with Pat as stand by, and their system was to make everyone bring possessions into the big bedroom (the one which Kay and I share), sort and fold them neatly – under Pat's quartermaster eye – then pass them over to Kay in order, books and boots and such things first, so that she could pack them methodically into the two big trunks.

This sounds perfectly simple, but there are always hitches and hold-ups. Jan produced a pair of shoes absolutely caked with mud, and had to be sent to clean them. Sally and I both seemed to have an alarming number of odd socks, until we found we'd each got about half a dozen of the others'. And Kay was the worst culprit of all, because she clean forgot

Under Pat's quartermaster eye

that she'd left her painting things downstairs, and remembered only when she'd reached the pyjama stage in packing.

By the time we'd got everything in, and Pat and Kay had fastened up (with the others of us sitting as heavily as we could on top), and Pat and Jan had done the roping, and Pat the labelling, it was dinnertime, and half of our last day had gone.

The afternoon we had reserved for saying good-bye to people and places. There would be no time for this tomorrow, for we would have to be off in the farm lorry almost before it was daylight, to catch the morning train from Windermere.

So, as soon as we'd done the after-dinner clearing, we made our round of the farm. We visited the cows in their byre, and Bobbin in his stable. We leaned in a row over the pigsty, and scratched the pigs just behind their ears till they grunted with complete satisfaction. Then we gathered up the eggs, and said a word to the birds in the fowl-houses in the little intak.

'Seem a bit bedraggled, don't they?' Kay said, looking at the row of rather miserable hens perched in the gloom inside and clucking in little throaty voices to themselves and each other.

'It's the melting snow and all this dampness they hate. They're complaining about their rheumatic twinges, I expect,' suggested Pat.

'Silly old things,' I scolded them. 'Why don't you move about a bit, and cheer yourselves up?'

'The cock's all right, though,' interrupted Jan. 'He's not frightened of a bit of weather.'

The great cock strode proudly up and down, and shook out his brilliant hackle feathers, and opened his beak in a lusty crow.

'Now that's what I call a decent good-bye!' declared Pat.

'And I think he said "Come back soon",' added Sally.

We went down the cart track through the meadow, and stopped to cast our eyes on the sheep that had been gathered there from the fells during the blizzard. They were certainly cheered by the change in the weather, and nosed and nibbled eagerly in the places where the thaw had thinned the snow.

We took the road down to Skelwith Bridge to see Farmer Wetherby and his wife. The dogs came all the way with us, bounding about our heels, running

ahead for a short distance, and then tearing back.
They always seemed to know when the end of a holiday had come, and never let us out of sight on the last
day.

At the Wetherbys' we had our usual welcome, and
sat round the kitchen fire, eating large slices of Mrs
Wetherby's fruit cake, and talking hard about what
we'd do next time.

It must have been about half past three as we came
back along the road from Skelwith Bridge – late afternoon when the month is January.

'Let's cut up on to the crags on Black Fell,' suggested Jan, 'and take a last look at everything.'

'What about our shoes?' Kay looked a bit doubtful. 'They'll get awfully wet in this smushy snow, and
they're the ones we're travelling in tomorrow.'

'Stuff them with newspaper and put them near to
the fire tonight,' said Pat. 'They'll dry out all right
before morning.'

So, half-way back along the road, we turned off to
the left, scrambled up the fellside to one of our view-
points, and had a most superb last look at all the
things that counted.

The sun was just going down through one or two
wispy bits of gold-fringed cloud, well to the south of
west, and the whole earth shone with the same burnished golden light. In spite of the thaw there was still
snow almost everywhere. We knew that the tops of
the fells would be covered for weeks, and that probably they would be shrouded in raging blizzards
many times before spring and summer really came.
But now they stood up mightily in a great circle,
shining, white, and beautiful, and we could pick out

Last look at all the things that counted

and name every one of them, all the way round from
Dow Crags and the Old Man through Wetherlam,
Crinkles, Bowfell, and the Langdales, to Helvellyn,
Fairfield, Dollywagon Pike, Ill Bell, and High Street.

We stood there, all five of us, just looking, and stor-
ing up memories to last through the long weeks when
we should be away.

'They look so high, and far away, and almost not
real,' I said. 'It's funny to think that some time next
summer we'll probably be lying on top of the very
highest of them, and panting from heat and thirst,
and sweltering in the sunshine.'

We came down from the crags just as the sun's last
rays set the fell-tops on fire, and burnished the odd
patches of green where the snow had melted. It was as
lovely as we'd ever seen it, but, for us, a sad moment.

and the procession across the farm-yard wasn't a very lively one.

'Oh, look!' exclaimed Sally (who was the tail). 'Look what I've found: two whites and a yellow!'

Kay turned back to where she was leaning over the little garden plot under the kitchen window, the plot that is always brilliant in summer with nasturtiums and scabious.

'Oh, Sally, what a find! Two snowdrops and an aconite, the very first. Isn't that clever of you!'

The rest of us doubled back to see what it was all about. Mr and Mrs Jenks came too, and Mr Tiggle followed behind.

'*Do* look what Sally's found,' said Kay, 'the very

'*And Easter means – High Tarn?*'

first snowdrops, just where the snow's melted. They must have been in flower while they were still covered over. I guess there'll be lots when the thaw really comes.'

'Snowdrops!' exclaimed Jan – the family optimist. 'Then that means spring – pretty nearly.'

'And spring, of course,' added Pat, 'means Easter.'

'And Easter,' I said, glancing rather shyly at Mr and Mrs Jenks, 'means – High Tarn?'

'Of *course* it does!' roared Mr Jenks, slapping his thigh with a tremendous gusto. 'Well, isn't it fine that we've all got something to look forward to?'

'*Indeed* it is,' agreed Mrs Jenks. 'And I'm sure that Mr Tiggle thinks so, too; don't you, puss?'

'Mi-aow!' said Mr Tiggle without hesitation. Which settled the matter quite definitely, and certainly to all our satisfactions.

If you have enjoyed this book and would like to know about others which we publish, why not join the Puffin Club? You will receive the club magazine, *Puffin Post*, four times a year and a smart badge and membership book. You will also be able to enter all the competitions. For details of cost and an application form, send a stamped addressed envelope to:

The Puffin Club Dept A
Penguin Books Limited
Bath Road
Harmondsworth
Middlesex